THE HARDY BOYS
THE NEW CASE FILES
Undercover Brothers
Based on the series by Franklin W. Dixon
BREAK-UP!
PAPERCUTZ™

THE HARDY BOYS GRAPHIC NOVELS FROM PAPERCUTZ

#1 "The Ocean of Osyria"

#2 "Identity Theft"

#3 "Mad House"

#4 "Malled"

#5 "Sea You, Sea Me!"

#6 "Hyde & Shriek"

#7 "The Opposite Numbers"

#8 "Board To Death"

#9 "To Die Or Not To Die?"

#10 "A Hardy Day's Night"

#11 "Abracadeath"

#12 "Dude Ranch O' Death!"

#13 "The Deadliest Stunt"

#14 "Haley Danielle's Top Eight!"

#15 "Live Free, Die Hardy!"

#16 "Shhhhhh!"

#17 "Word Up!"

#18 "D.A.N.G.E.R Spells the Hangman"

#19 "Chaos at 30,000 Feet"

#20 "Deadly Strategy"

$7.95 each in paperback, $12.95 each in hardcover except #20, $8.99pb/$13.99hc.
Available through all booksellers.

See more at www.papercutz.com

Or you can order through us: please add $4.00 for postage and handling for the first book, and add $1.00 for each additional book. Please make check payable to NBM Publishing. Send to: Papercutz, 1200 County Rd., Rte 523, Flemington, NJ 08222 or call 800 886 1223 (9-6 EST M-F) MC-Visa-Amex accepted

THE HARDY BOYS

THE NEW CASE FILES

Undercover Brothers

BREAK-UP!

GERRY CONWAY
Writer

PAULO HENRIQUE
Artist

Based on the series by FRANKLIN W. DIXON

PAPERCUTZ™
New York

"Break-Up"
GERRY CONWAY - Writer
PAULO HENRIQUE - Artist
LAURIE E. SMITH - Colorist
BRYAN SENKA - Letterer
SHELLY STERNER & CHRIS NELSON - Production
MICHAEL PETRANEK - Associate Editor
JIM SALICRUP
Editor-in-Chief

ISBN: 978-1-59707-242-7 paperback edition
ISBN: 978-1-59707-243-4 hardcover edition
Copyright © 2011 by Simon & Schuster, Inc. Published by arrangement with
Aladdin Paperbacks, an imprint of Simon & Schuster Children's Publishing Division.

Printed in China
January 2011 by O.G. Printing Productions, LTD.
Unit 2 & 3, 5/F Lemmi Centre
50 Hoi Yen Road
Kwon Tong, Kowloon

Distributed by Macmillan.
First Printing

CHAPTER ONE:
ANOTHER FINE MESS

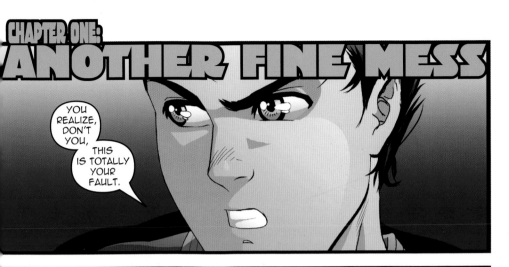

YOU REALIZE, DON'T YOU, THIS IS TOTALLY YOUR FAULT.

MY FAULT? IF WE'D HANDLED THIS THE WAY *I* WANTED, WE'D BE REPORTING IN TO A.T.A.C.* HOW WE'D SOLVED ANOTHER CASE RIGHT ABOUT NOW.

BUT NO--

*AMERICAN TEENS AGAINST CRIME

REALLY, JOE? YOU REALLY THINK THIS IS THE TIME TO DEBATE DIFFERENT METHODS OF *INVESTIGATING* CRIMES?

WHY *NOT*, FRANK?

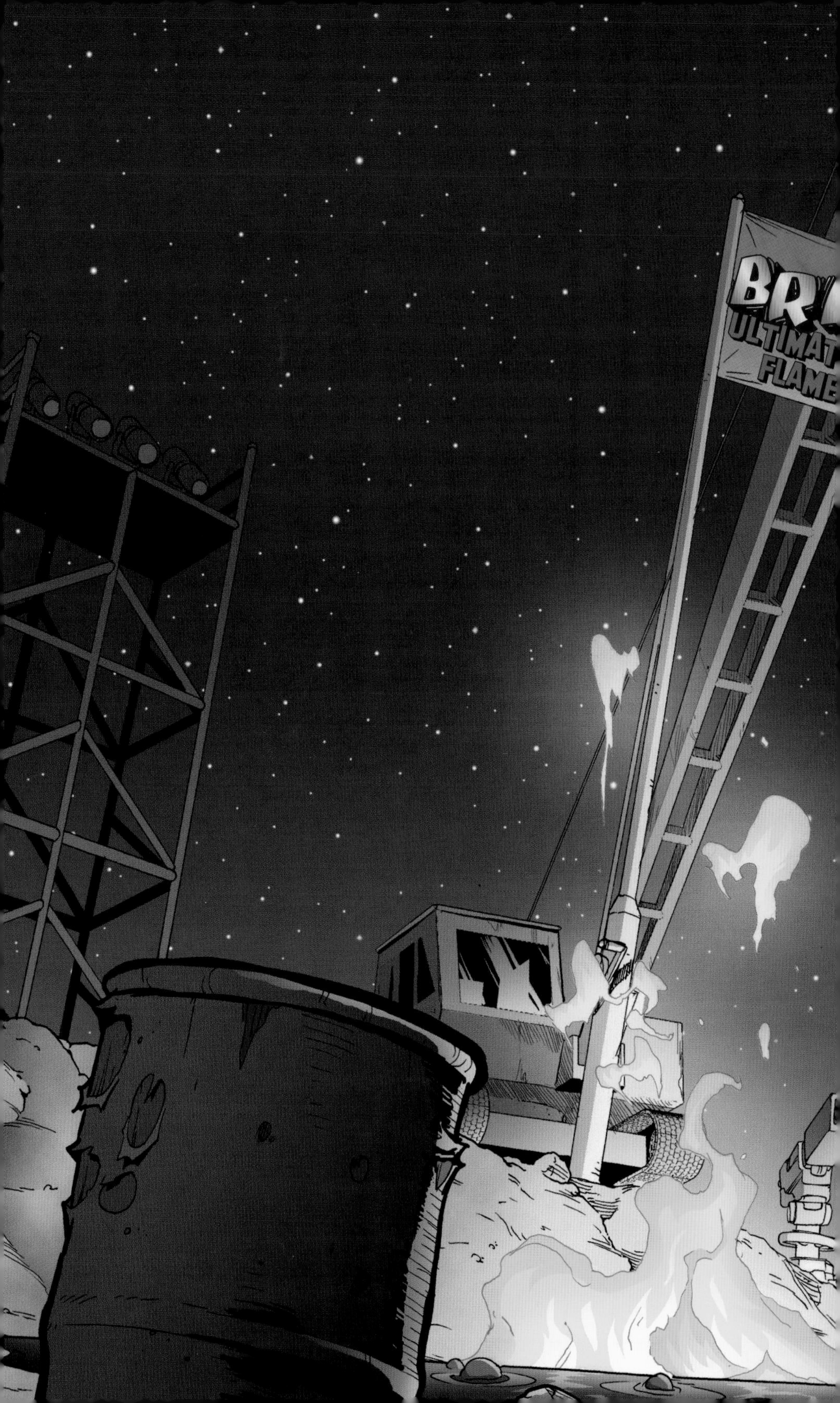

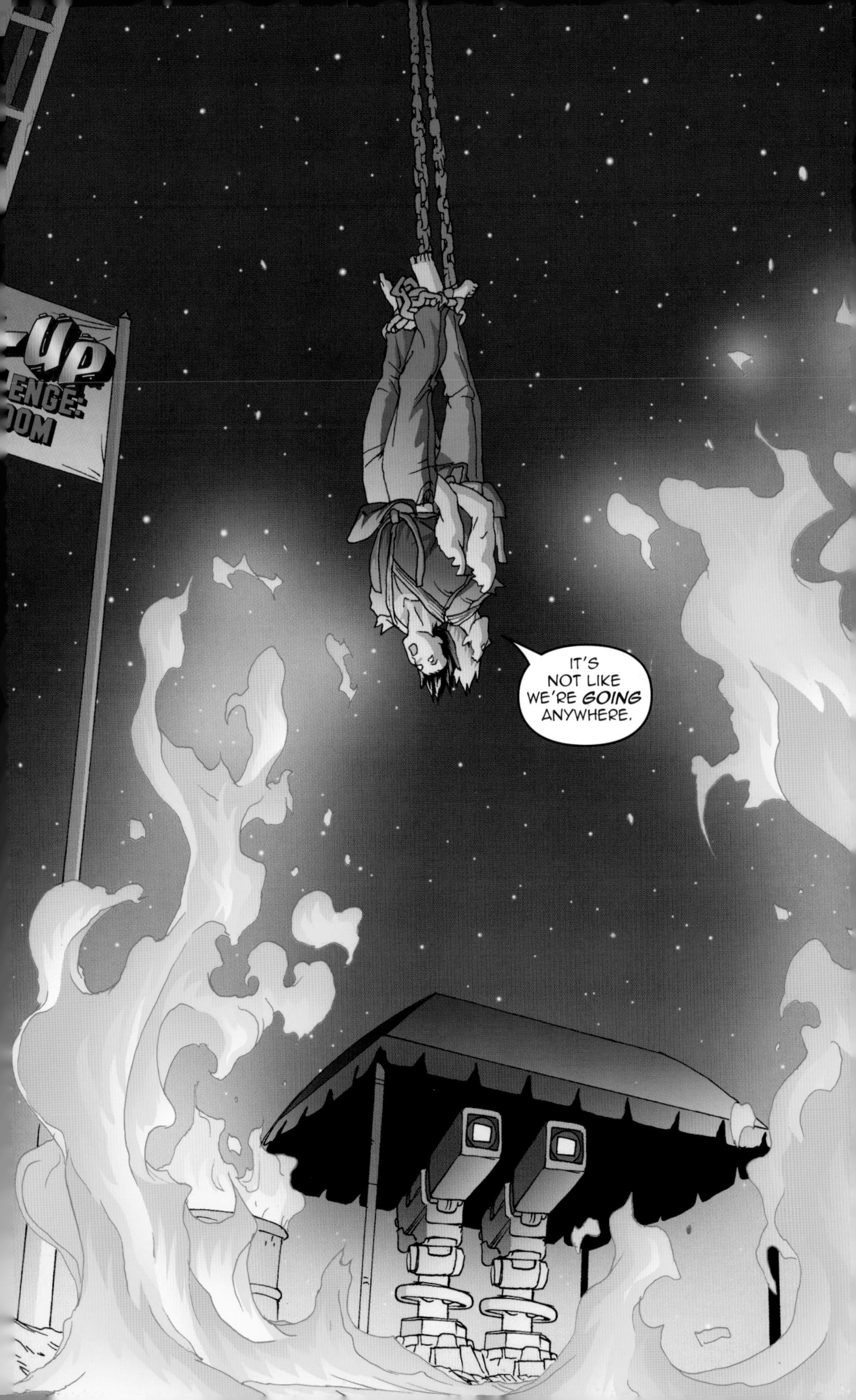
IT'S NOT LIKE WE'RE *GOING* ANYWHERE.

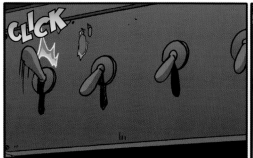

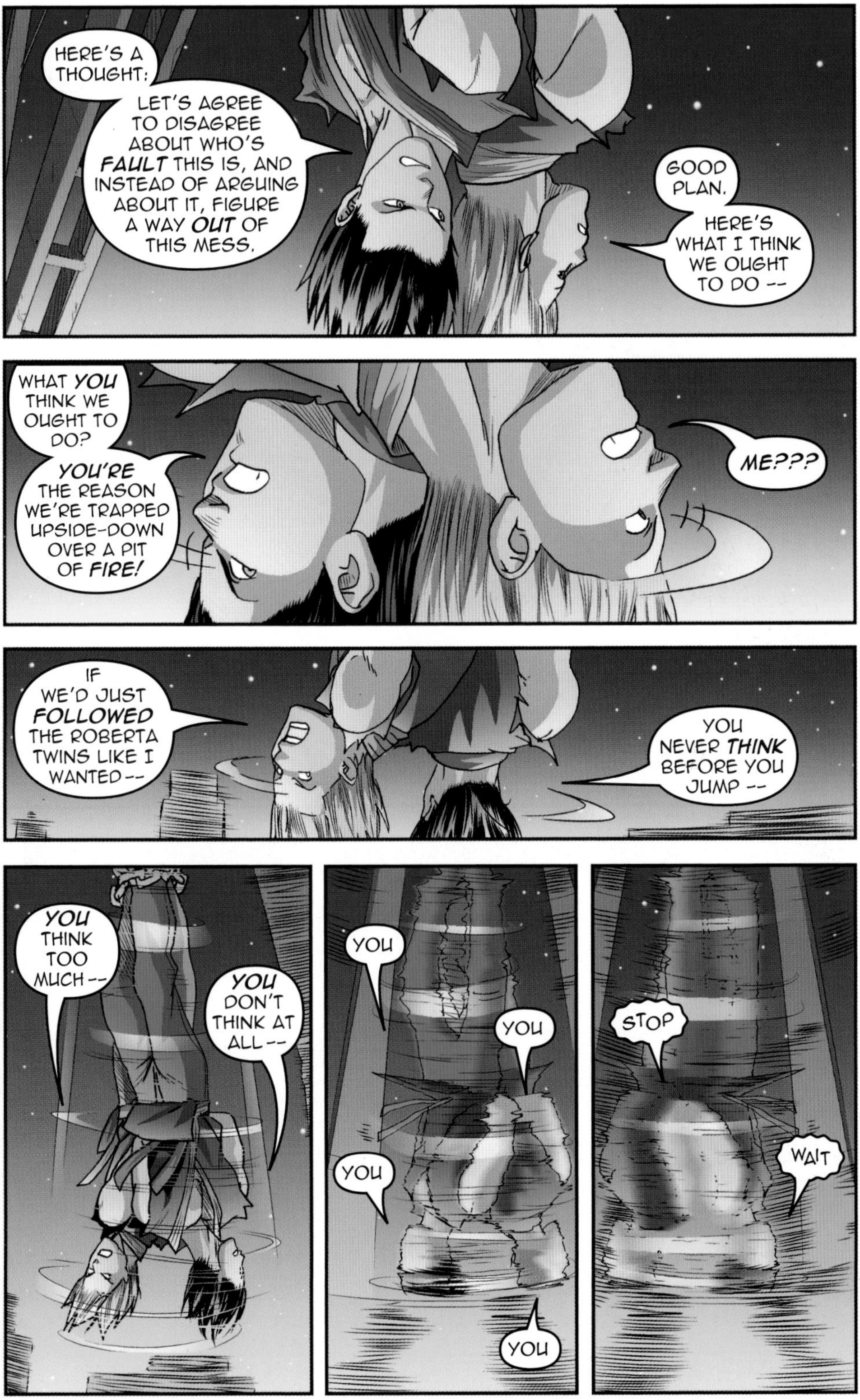
HERE'S A THOUGHT:
LET'S AGREE TO DISAGREE ABOUT WHO'S FAULT THIS IS, AND INSTEAD OF ARGUING ABOUT IT, FIGURE A WAY OUT OF THIS MESS.
GOOD PLAN.
HERE'S WHAT I THINK WE OUGHT TO DO --
WHAT YOU THINK WE OUGHT TO DO?
YOU'RE THE REASON WE'RE TRAPPED UPSIDE-DOWN OVER A PIT OF FIRE!
ME???
IF WE'D JUST FOLLOWED THE ROBERTA TWINS LIKE I WANTED --
YOU NEVER THINK BEFORE YOU JUMP --
YOU THINK TOO MUCH --
YOU DON'T THINK AT ALL --
YOU
YOU
YOU
YOU
STOP
WAIT

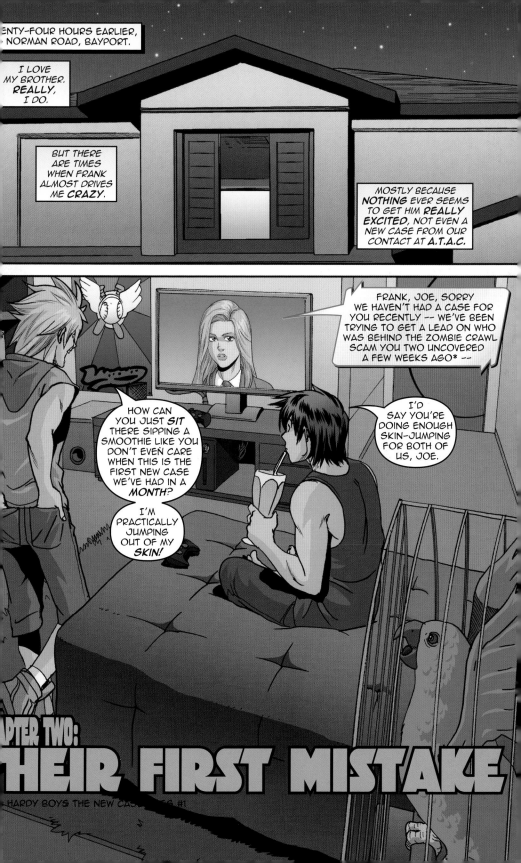

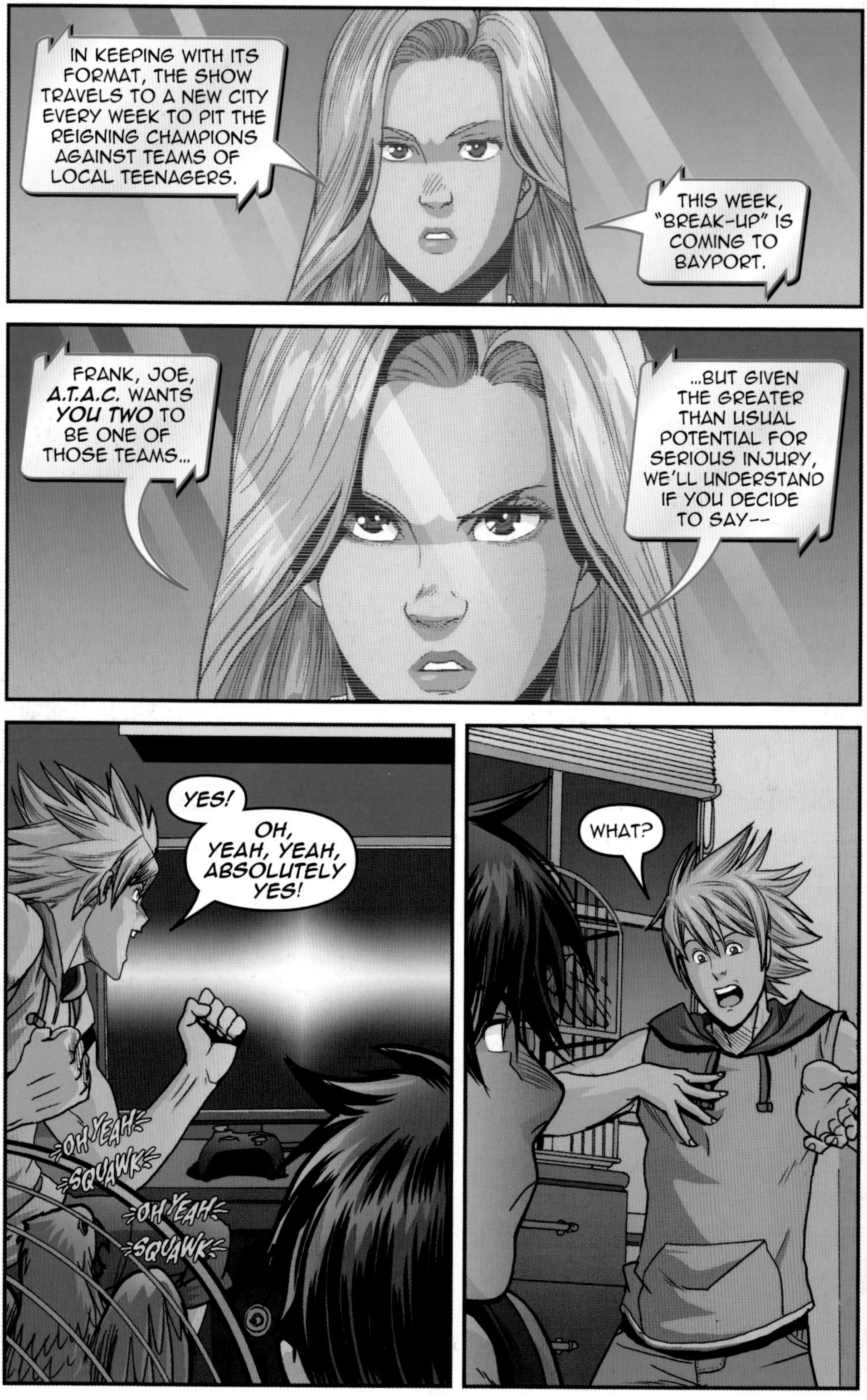
IN KEEPING WITH ITS FORMAT, THE SHOW TRAVELS TO A NEW CITY EVERY WEEK TO PIT THE REIGNING CHAMPIONS AGAINST TEAMS OF LOCAL TEENAGERS.
THIS WEEK, "BREAK-UP" IS COMING TO BAYPORT.
FRANK, JOE, A.T.A.C. WANTS *YOU TWO* TO BE ONE OF THOSE TEAMS...
...BUT GIVEN THE GREATER THAN USUAL POTENTIAL FOR SERIOUS INJURY, WE'LL UNDERSTAND IF YOU DECIDE TO SAY--
YES!
OH, YEAH, YEAH, ABSOLUTELY YES!
OH YEAH
SQUAWK
OH YEAH
SQUAWK
WHAT?

NOW.

TYPICAL JOE. ALWAYS READY TO RUSH INTO ACTION, WITHOUT A PLAN --

-- JUST BARGE AHEAD AND HOPE FOR THE BEST.

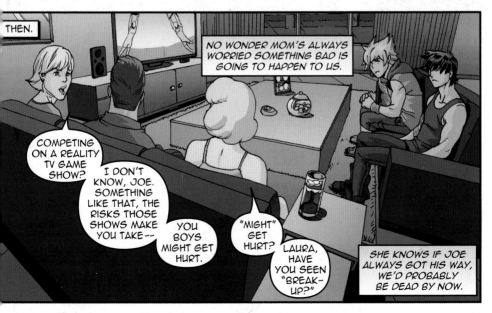

THEN.

NO WONDER MOM'S ALWAYS WORRIED SOMETHING BAD IS GOING TO HAPPEN TO US.

COMPETING ON A REALITY TV GAME SHOW?

I DON'T KNOW, JOE. SOMETHING LIKE THAT, THE RISKS THOSE SHOWS MAKE YOU TAKE--

YOU BOYS MIGHT GET HURT.

"MIGHT" GET HURT?

LAURA, HAVE YOU SEEN "BREAK-UP?"

SHE KNOWS IF JOE ALWAYS GOT HIS WAY, WE'D PROBABLY BE DEAD BY NOW.

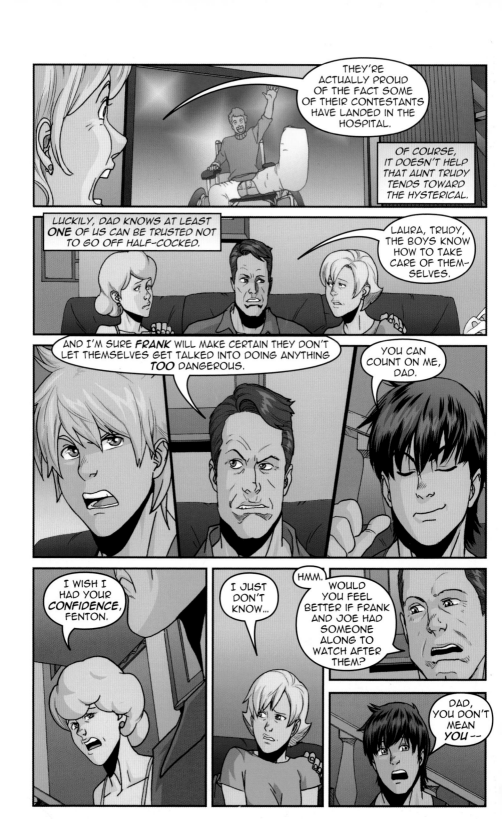

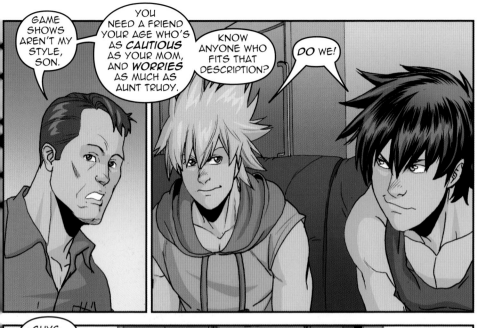

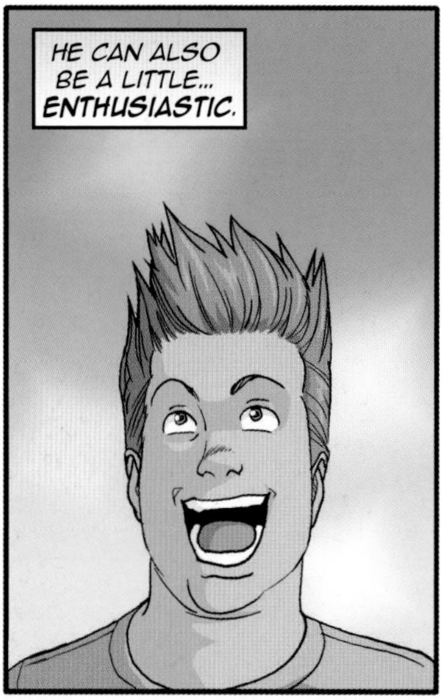
HE CAN ALSO BE A LITTLE... ENTHUSIASTIC.

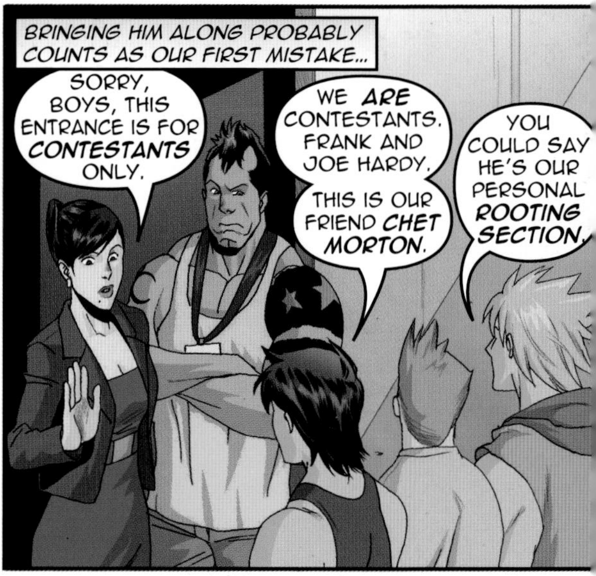
BRINGING HIM ALONG PROBABLY COUNTS AS OUR FIRST MISTAKE...
SORRY, BOYS, THIS ENTRANCE IS FOR CONTESTANTS ONLY.
WE ARE CONTESTANTS. FRANK AND JOE HARDY.
THIS IS OUR FRIEND CHET MORTON.
YOU COULD SAY HE'S OUR PERSONAL ROOTING SECTION.

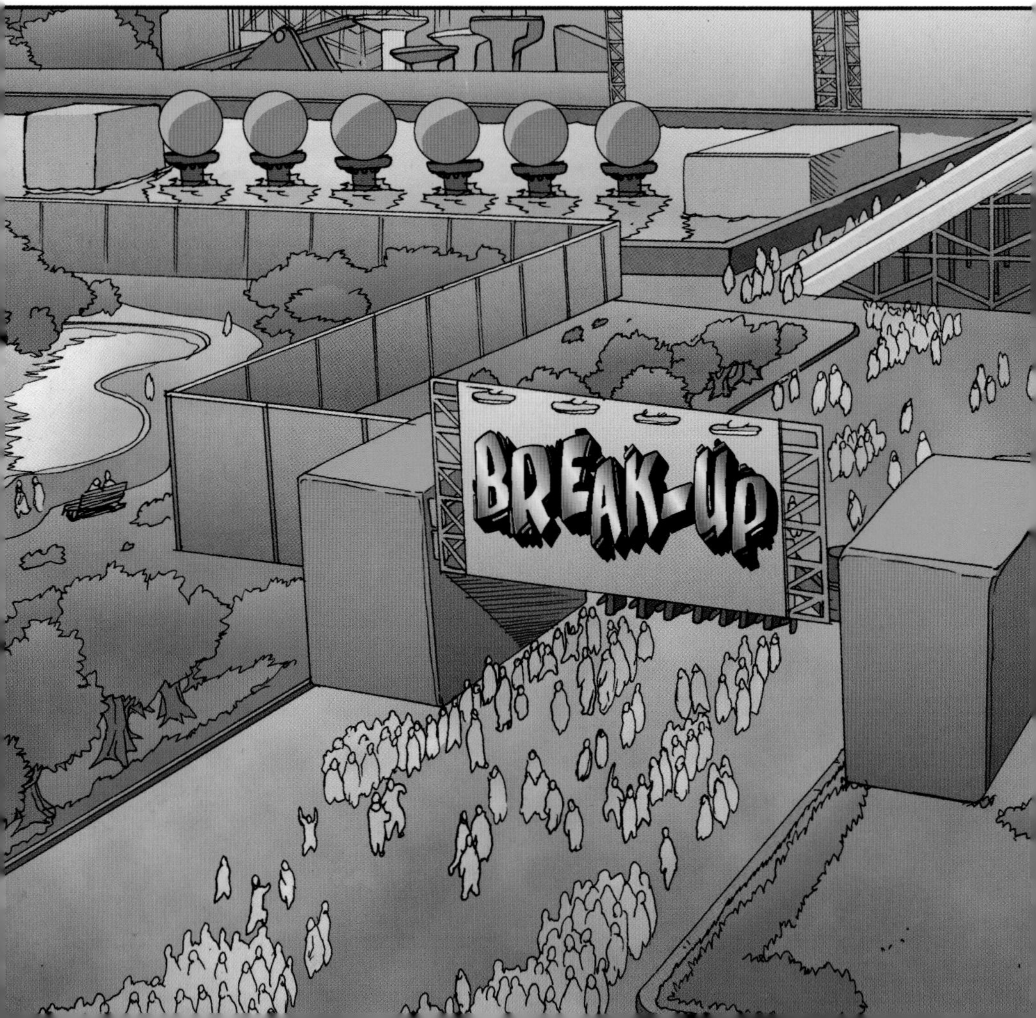
BREAK-UP

THAT GUY MIKE WALLABY ALMOST SOUNDS LIKE HE *EXPECTS* SOMETHING TO GO WRONG.

"ANYTHING HAPPENS, IT'S ON YOUR HEAD."

WHAT ABOUT THE PRODUCER, LINDA HUNT? "RULES ARE MADE TO BE BROKEN."

PRETTY *CASUAL* ATTITUDE FOR SUCH A DANGEROUS SHOW --

?

GOD WILL *PUNISH* YOU!

TELEVISION IS VANITY, COMPETITION FOR WORLDLY RECOGNITION IS AN *AFFRONT* TO THE LORD!

SECURITY

YOU'RE BUILDING A *TOWER OF BABEL*, AND GOD'S WRATH WILL SEND IT *CRASHING DOWN!*

WHO IS THAT, AND *WHAT* RUBBER-WALL ACADEMY LET *HIM* GRADUATE?

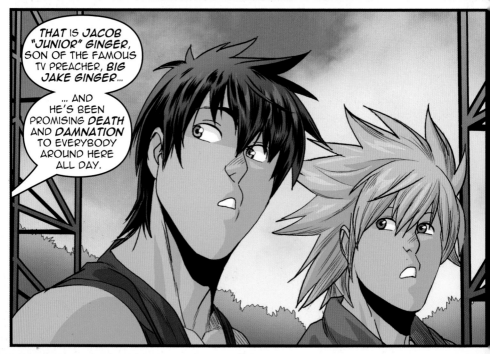

THAT IS JACOB *"JUNIOR"* GINGER, SON OF THE FAMOUS TV PREACHER, *BIG JAKE GINGER...*

... AND HE'S BEEN PROMISING *DEATH* AND *DAMNATION* TO EVERYBODY AROUND HERE ALL DAY.

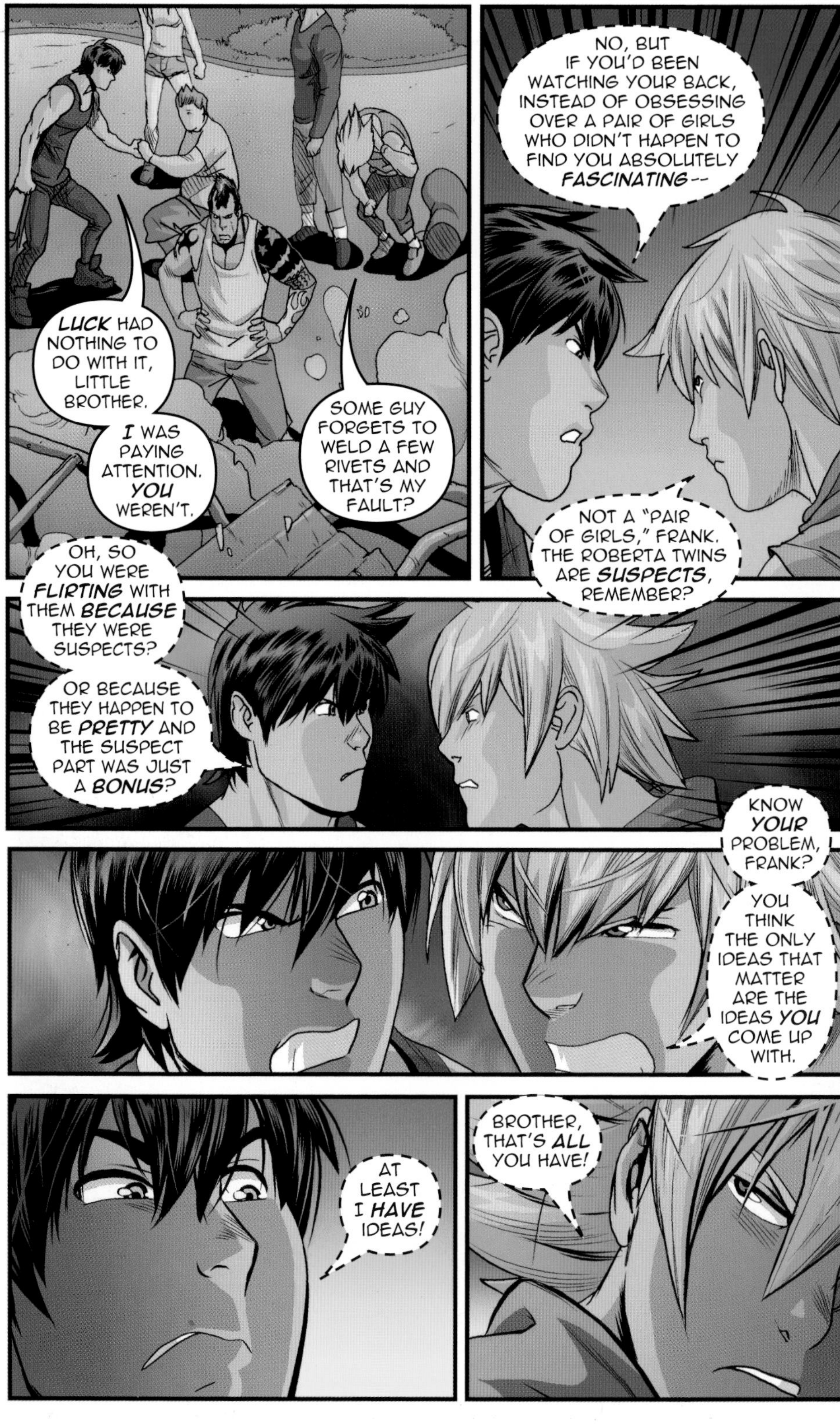
LUCK HAD NOTHING TO DO WITH IT, LITTLE BROTHER.
I WAS PAYING ATTENTION. YOU WEREN'T.
SOME GUY FORGETS TO WELD A FEW RIVETS AND THAT'S MY FAULT?
NO, BUT IF YOU'D BEEN WATCHING YOUR BACK, INSTEAD OF OBSESSING OVER A PAIR OF GIRLS WHO DIDN'T HAPPEN TO FIND YOU ABSOLUTELY FASCINATING--
NOT A "PAIR OF GIRLS," FRANK. THE ROBERTA TWINS ARE SUSPECTS, REMEMBER?
OH, SO YOU WERE FLIRTING WITH THEM BECAUSE THEY WERE SUSPECTS?
OR BECAUSE THEY HAPPEN TO BE PRETTY AND THE SUSPECT PART WAS JUST A BONUS?
KNOW YOUR PROBLEM, FRANK?
YOU THINK THE ONLY IDEAS THAT MATTER ARE THE IDEAS YOU COME UP WITH.
AT LEAST I HAVE IDEAS!
BROTHER, THAT'S ALL YOU HAVE!

UH, GUYS... ARE YOU OKAY?

YEAH, SURE, WE'RE FINE.

THE QUESTION IS -- WHAT HAPPENED TO THAT *SCAFFOLDING*? WHY DID IT *COLLAPSE* LIKE THAT?

WISH I KNEW, MATES.

I KEEP A CLOSE WATCH ON *CONSTRUCTION* -- THAT'S MY JOB -- AND I COULDA *SWORN* THAT SCAFFOLD WAS SAFE AS HOUSES.

ARE YOU *KIDDING* ME?

WHAT IF THAT HAPPENED WHILE YOU WERE TAPING A SHOW? SOMEBODY COULD'VE BEEN *KILLED*.

HEY, YOUR PARENTS SIGNED A *RELEASE*. WOULD'VE MADE *GREAT TV*.

ACCIDENTS HAPPEN, MIKE.

THAT'S WHY WE HAVE *INSURANCE*.

BUT SINCE NO ONE WAS HURT, WHY *WORRY* ABOUT IT?

GET THEM READY, MIKE. WE START TAPING IN AN HOUR.

JOE... LOOK AT LINDA HUNT'S HAND...

DO YOU SEE WHAT I SEE?

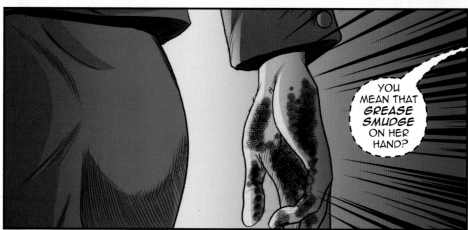

YOU MEAN THAT *GREASE SMUDGE* ON HER HAND?

SOMEBODY MADE THAT SCAFFOLDING CRASH.

WHOEVER DID IT *MIGHT* HAVE GOTTEN THEIR HANDS DIRTY.

ONE OF US OUGHT TO KEEP AN EYE ON MS. GREASE-MONKEY PRODUCER LADY.

I NOMINATE *ME*.

GUYS, THEY WANT YOU TO GET READY--

HARDYS! OVER HERE OR YOU'RE OUT OF THE GAME!

STALL THE MAN, FRANK.

I'LL CATCH UP WITH YOU IN A FEW MINUTES.

JOE-- NO--

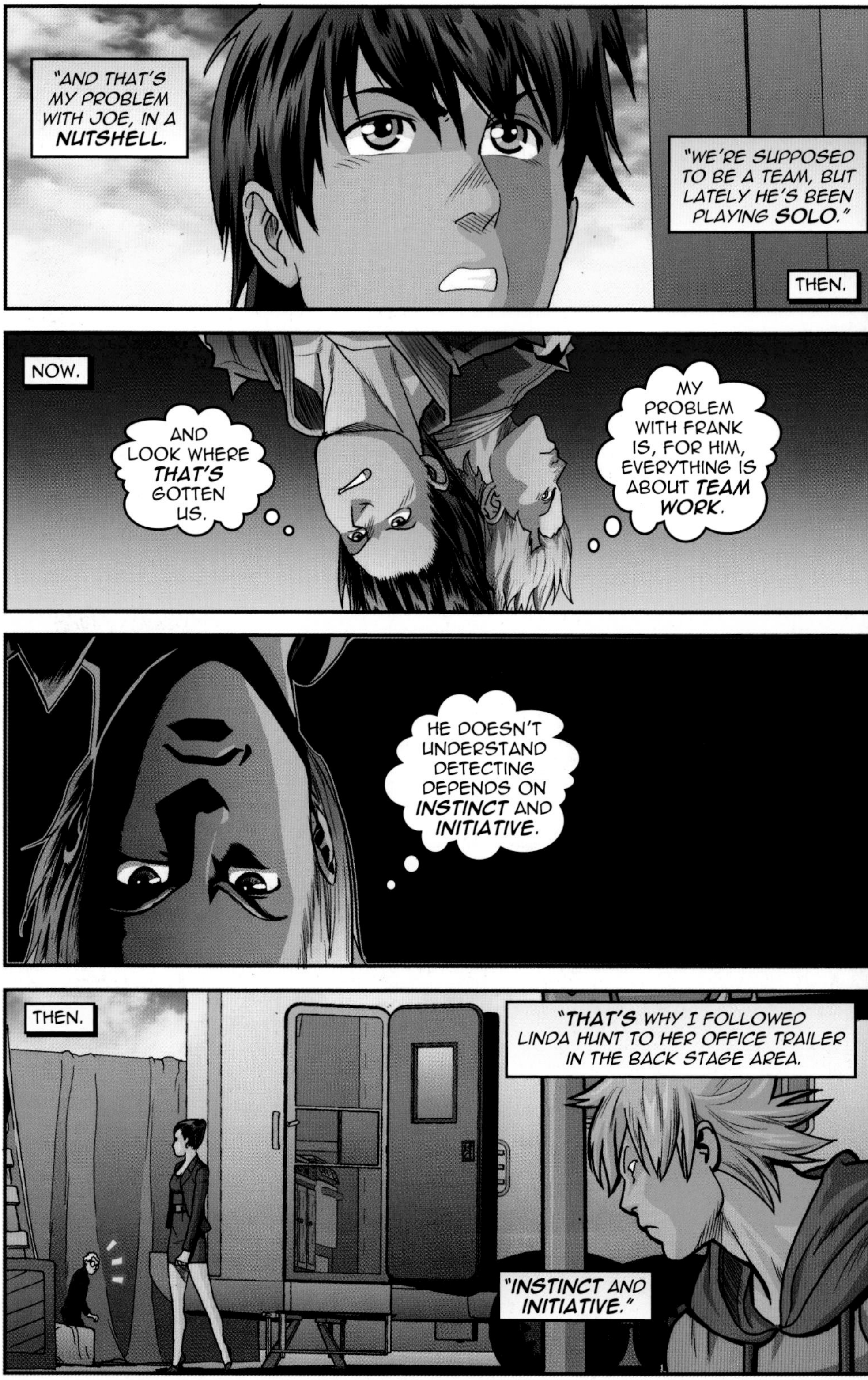
"AND THAT'S MY PROBLEM WITH JOE, IN A NUTSHELL.
"WE'RE SUPPOSED TO BE A TEAM, BUT LATELY HE'S BEEN PLAYING SOLO."
THEN.
NOW.
AND LOOK WHERE THAT'S GOTTEN US.
MY PROBLEM WITH FRANK IS, FOR HIM, EVERYTHING IS ABOUT TEAM WORK.
HE DOESN'T UNDERSTAND DETECTING DEPENDS ON INSTINCT AND INITIATIVE.
THEN.
"THAT'S WHY I FOLLOWED LINDA HUNT TO HER OFFICE TRAILER IN THE BACK STAGE AREA.
"INSTINCT AND INITIATIVE."

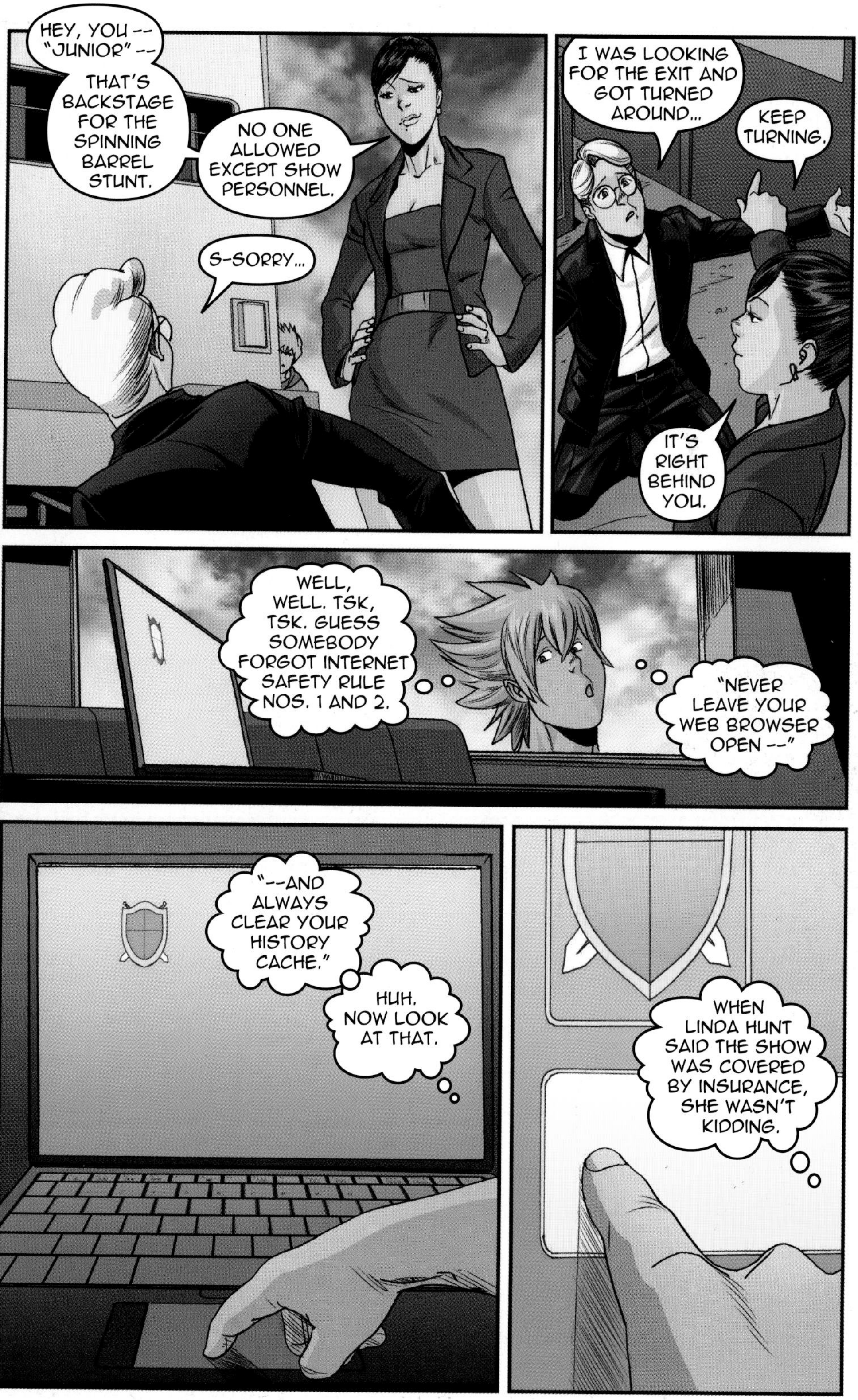
HEY, YOU -- "JUNIOR" --
THAT'S BACKSTAGE FOR THE SPINNING BARREL STUNT.
NO ONE ALLOWED EXCEPT SHOW PERSONNEL.
S-SORRY...
I WAS LOOKING FOR THE EXIT AND GOT TURNED AROUND...
KEEP TURNING.
IT'S RIGHT BEHIND YOU.
WELL, WELL. TSK, TSK. GUESS SOMEBODY FORGOT INTERNET SAFETY RULE NOS. 1 AND 2.
"NEVER LEAVE YOUR WEB BROWSER OPEN --"
"--AND ALWAYS CLEAR YOUR HISTORY CACHE."
HUH. NOW LOOK AT THAT.
WHEN LINDA HUNT SAID THE SHOW WAS COVERED BY INSURANCE, SHE WASN'T KIDDING.

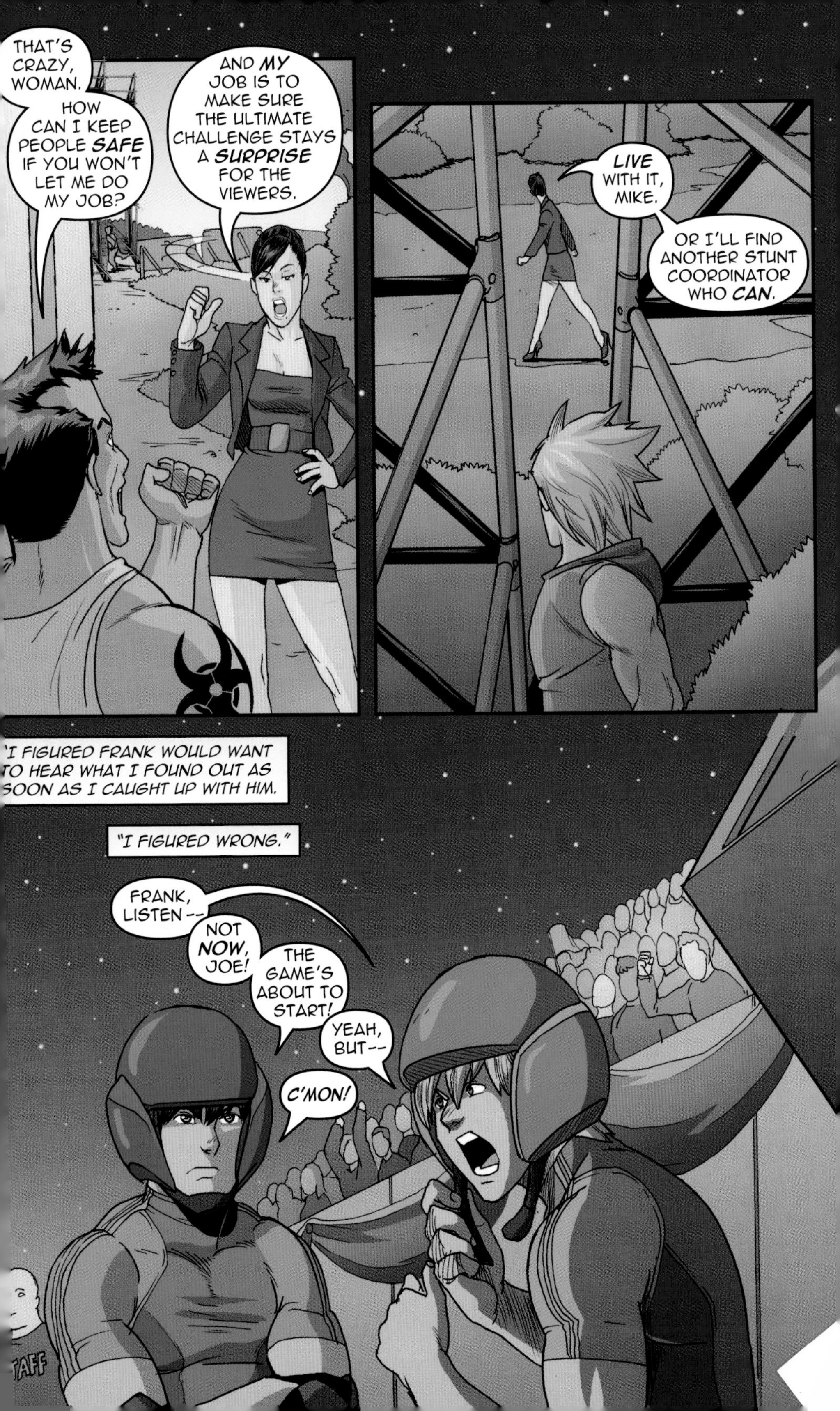
THAT'S CRAZY, WOMAN.
HOW CAN I KEEP PEOPLE SAFE IF YOU WON'T LET ME DO MY JOB?
AND MY JOB IS TO MAKE SURE THE ULTIMATE CHALLENGE STAYS A SURPRISE FOR THE VIEWERS.
LIVE WITH IT, MIKE.
OR I'LL FIND ANOTHER STUNT COORDINATOR WHO CAN.
"I FIGURED FRANK WOULD WANT TO HEAR WHAT I FOUND OUT AS SOON AS I CAUGHT UP WITH HIM.
"I FIGURED WRONG."
FRANK, LISTEN --
NOT NOW, JOE!
THE GAME'S ABOUT TO START!
YEAH, BUT--
C'MON!

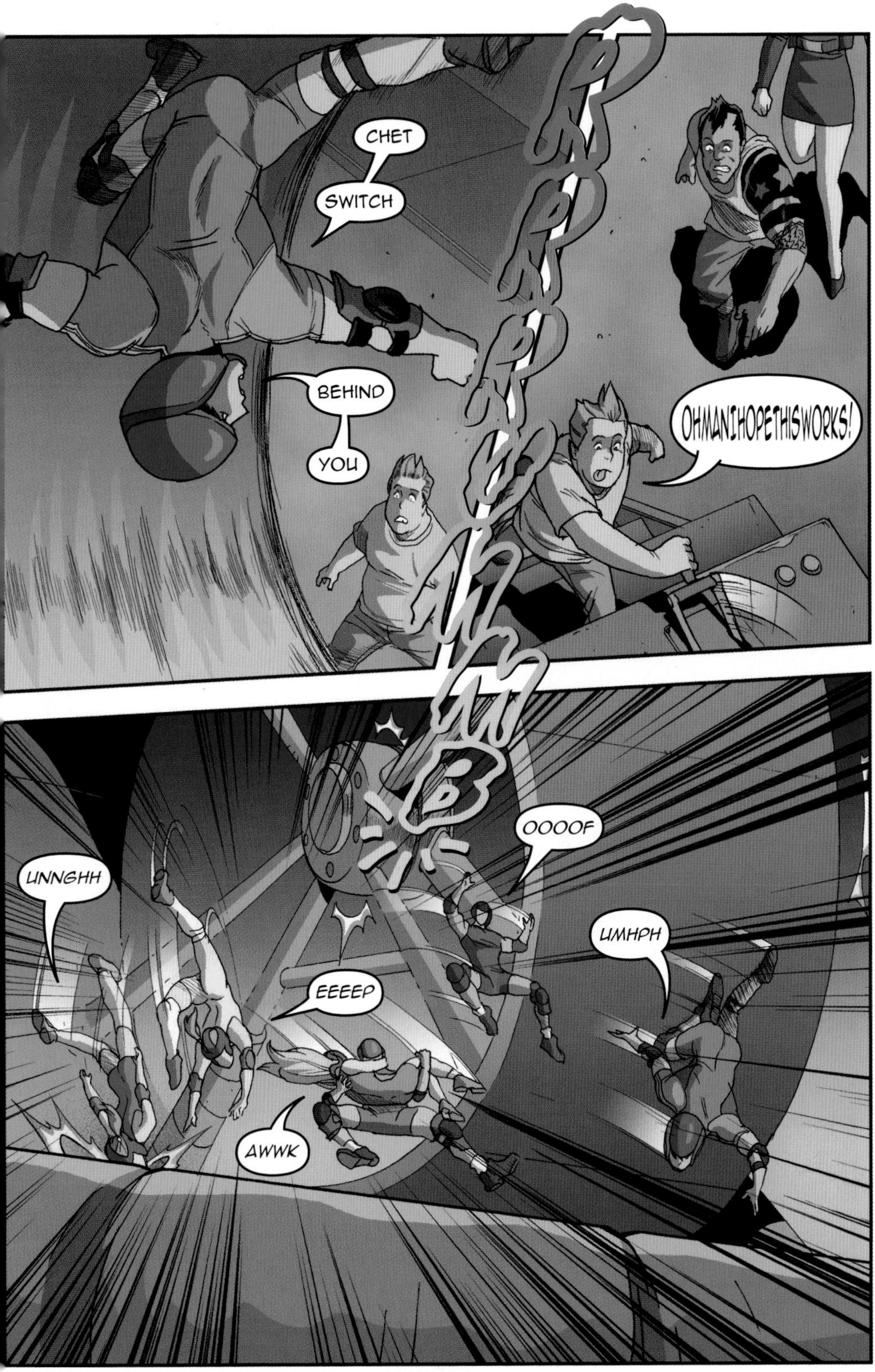
CHET
SWITCH
BEHIND
YOU
OHMANIHOPETHISWORKS!
OOOOF
UNNGHH
UMHPH
EEEEP
AWWK

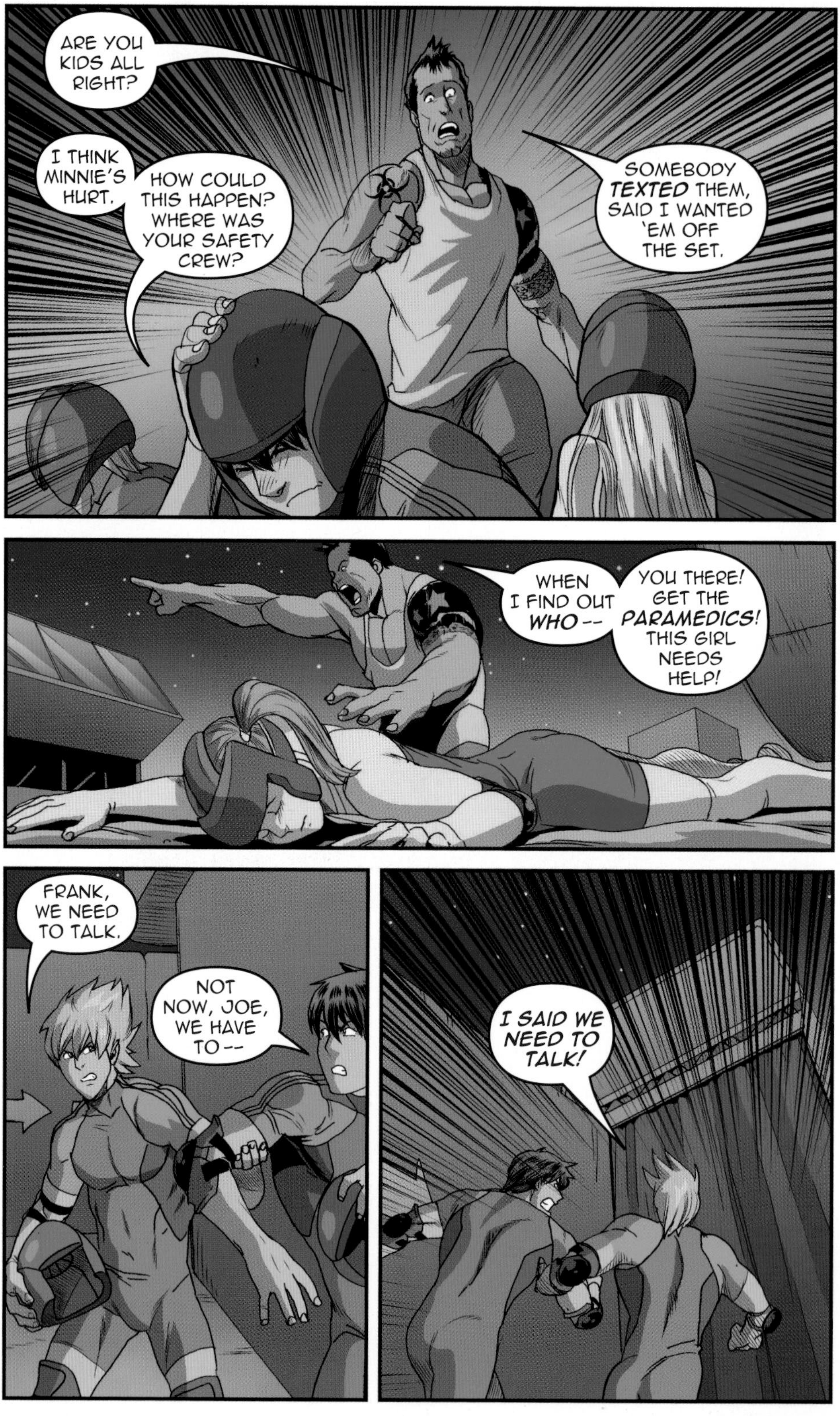
ARE YOU KIDS ALL RIGHT?
I THINK MINNIE'S HURT.
HOW COULD THIS HAPPEN? WHERE WAS YOUR SAFETY CREW?
SOMEBODY TEXTED THEM, SAID I WANTED 'EM OFF THE SET.
WHEN I FIND OUT WHO --
YOU THERE! GET THE PARAMEDICS! THIS GIRL NEEDS HELP!
FRANK, WE NEED TO TALK.
NOT NOW, JOE, WE HAVE TO --
I SAID WE NEED TO TALK!

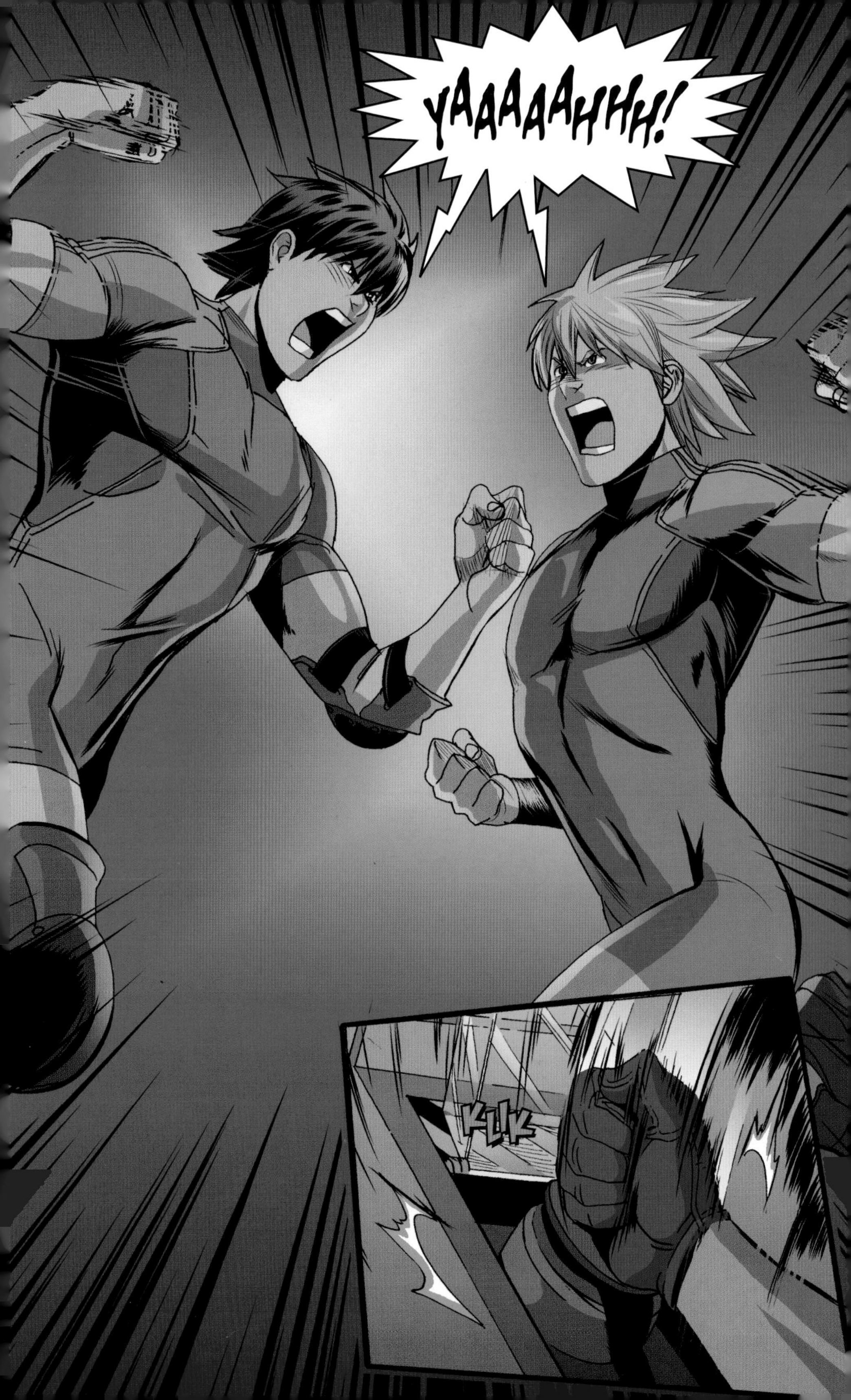
YAAAAAHHH!
KLIK

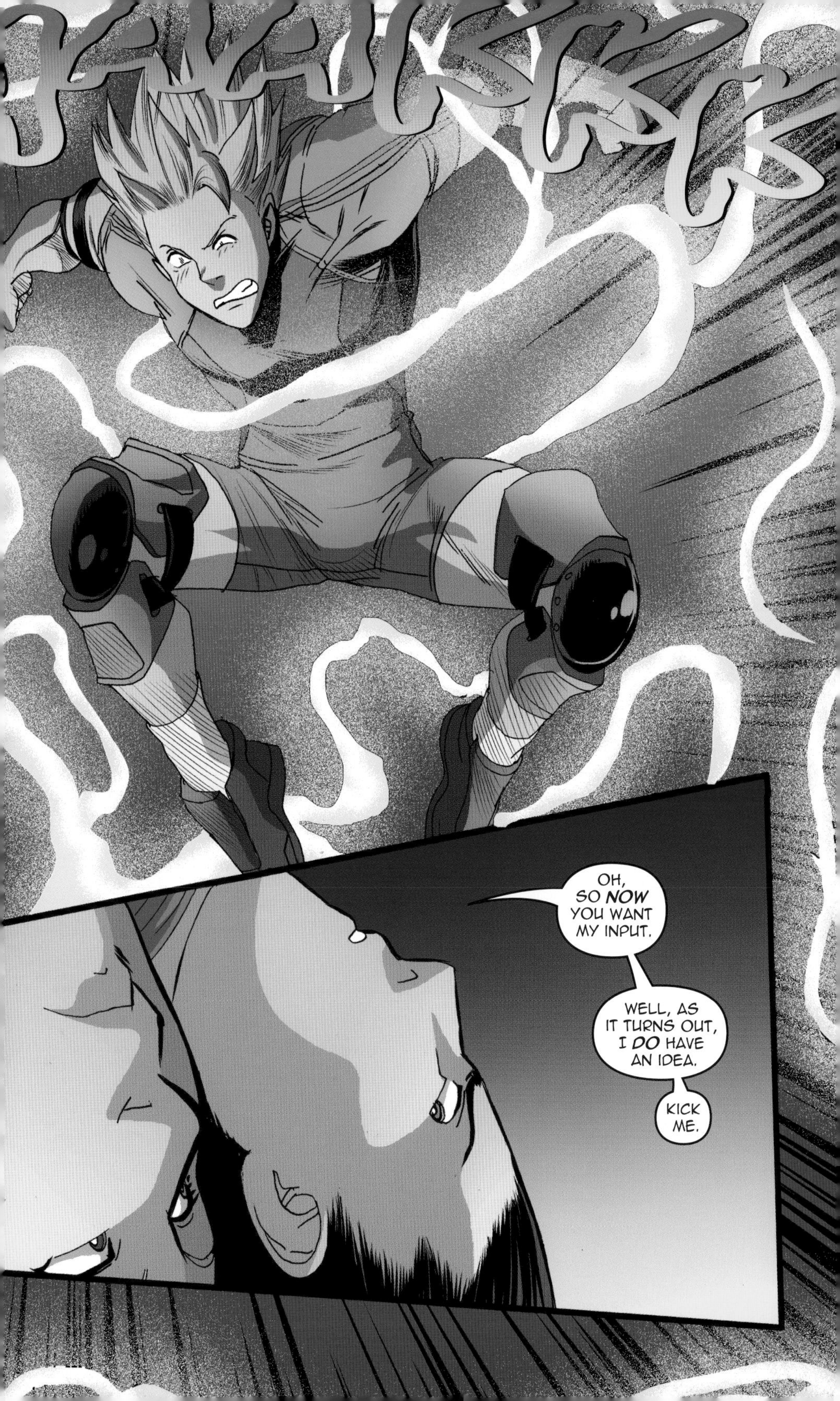
OH, SO NOW YOU WANT MY INPUT.
WELL, AS IT TURNS OUT, I DO HAVE AN IDEA.
KICK ME.

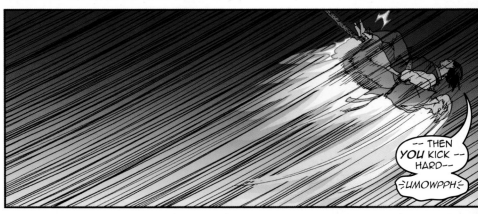

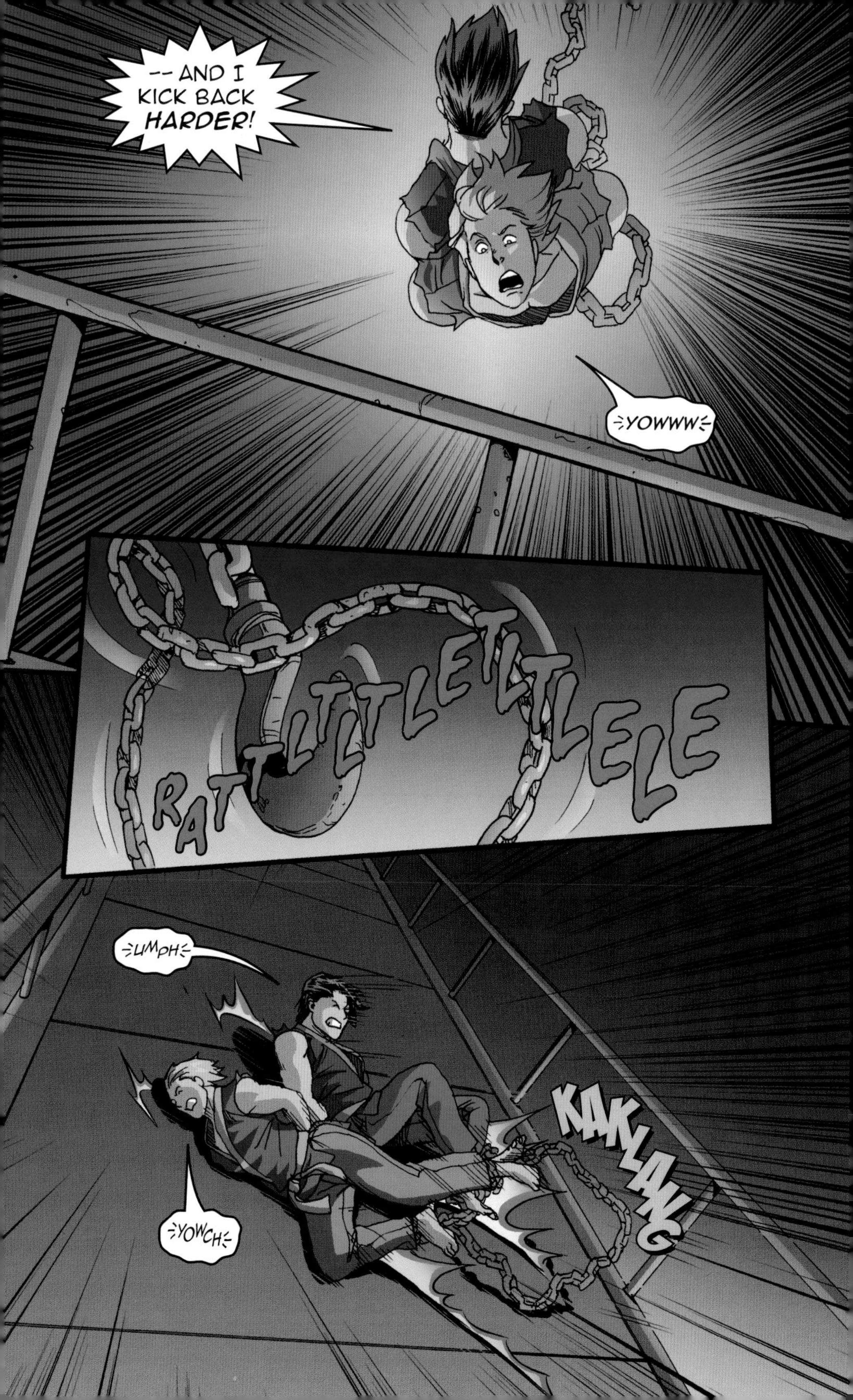
-- AND I KICK BACK HARDER!
YOWWW
RATTTLTTLTLETLTLELE
UMPH
KAKLANG
YOWCH

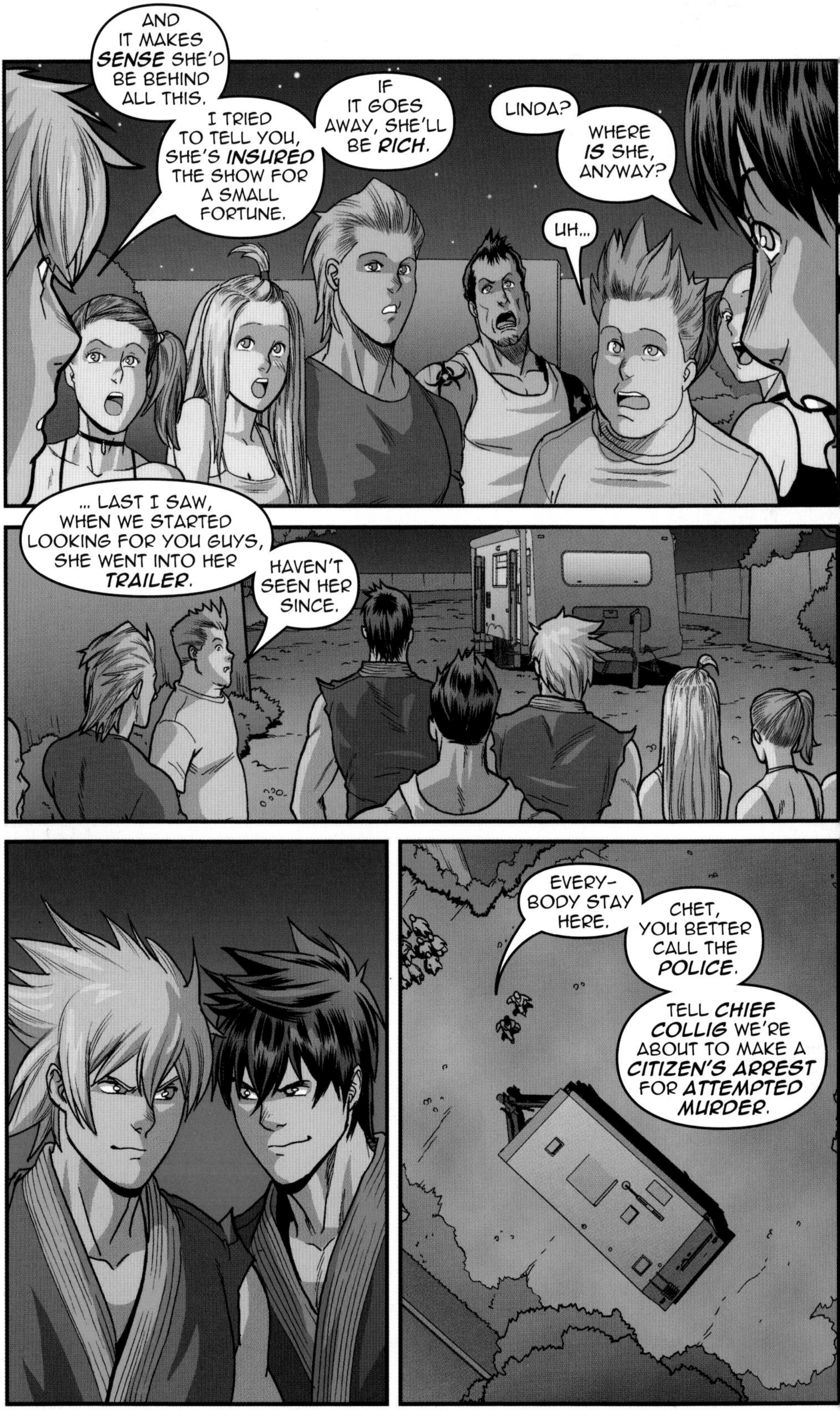
AND IT MAKES SENSE SHE'D BE BEHIND ALL THIS.
I TRIED TO TELL YOU, SHE'S INSURED THE SHOW FOR A SMALL FORTUNE.
IF IT GOES AWAY, SHE'LL BE RICH.
LINDA?
WHERE IS SHE, ANYWAY?
UH...
... LAST I SAW, WHEN WE STARTED LOOKING FOR YOU GUYS, SHE WENT INTO HER TRAILER.
HAVEN'T SEEN HER SINCE.
EVERY-BODY STAY HERE.
CHET, YOU BETTER CALL THE POLICE.
TELL CHIEF COLLIG WE'RE ABOUT TO MAKE A CITIZEN'S ARREST FOR ATTEMPTED MURDER.

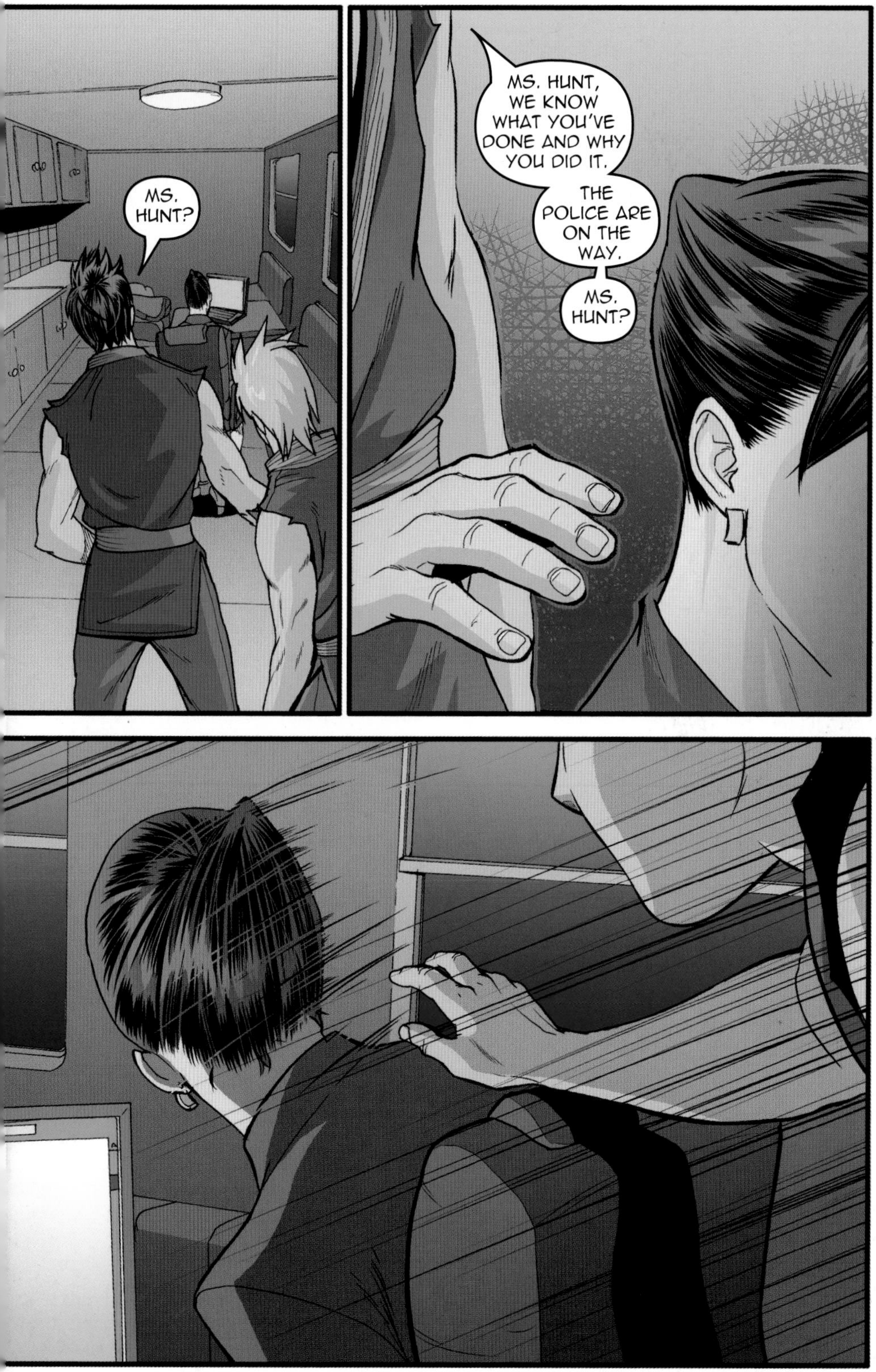

MS. HUNT?
MS. HUNT, WE KNOW WHAT YOU'VE DONE AND WHY YOU DID IT.
THE POLICE ARE ON THE WAY.
MS. HUNT?

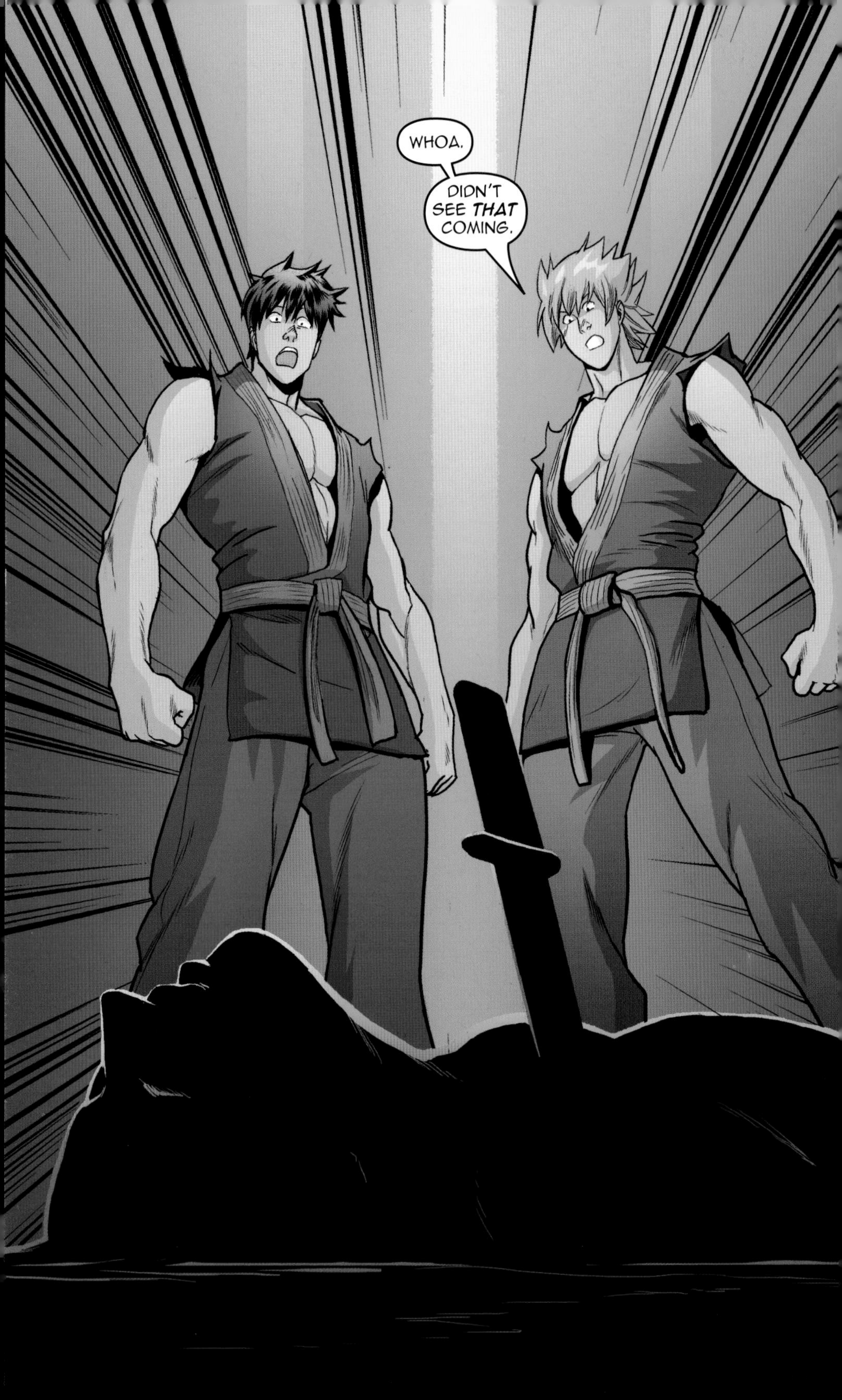
WHOA.
DIDN'T SEE THAT COMING.

176 NORMAN ROAD, BAYPORT.

THE HARDY HOUSE.

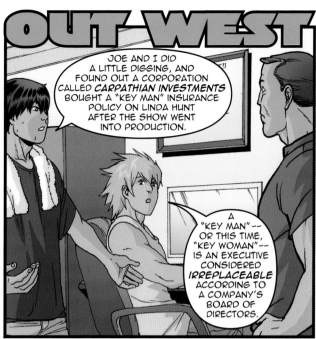

JOE AND I DID A LITTLE DIGGING, AND FOUND OUT A CORPORATION CALLED *CARPATHIAN INVESTMENTS* BOUGHT A "KEY MAN" INSURANCE POLICY ON LINDA HUNT AFTER THE SHOW WENT INTO PRODUCTION.

A "KEY MAN" -- OR THIS TIME, "KEY WOMAN"-- IS AN EXECUTIVE CONSIDERED *IRREPLACEABLE* ACCORDING TO A COMPANY'S BOARD OF DIRECTORS.

TURNS OUT LINDA HUNT WASN'T THE *ONLY* ONE WHO HAD MULTI-MILLION DOLLAR INSURANCE ON THE SHOW *"BREAK-UP."*

THE ASSUMPTION IS, IF THE "KEY" MAN OR WOMAN DIES, THE COMPANY GOES BANKRUPT.

"KEY MAN" INSURANCE *PROTECTS* THE COMPANY'S OWNER.

AND IF THE "KEY WOMAN" IN THIS CASE WERE ABOUT TO BE *ARRESTED* FOR ATTEMPTED MURDER--

--KILLING HER TO COLLECT THE INSURANCE WOULD BE ONE SURE WAY FOR AN INVESTOR TO GET HIS, HER, OR ITS *MONEY* BACK.

FENTON, BOYS -- *DINNER* TIME.

FRANK AND JOE, DON'T KEEP YOUR MOTHER WAITING!

WHICH BEGS THE QUESTION -- WHO OR WHAT IS *CARPATHIAN INVESTMENTS*?

SO FAR AS WE CAN FIND OUT, *NOBODY KNOWS*.

JOE'S EXAGGERATING, BUT NOT BY MUCH.

-- REGISTERED *ANONYMOUSLY* IN THE *CAYMAN ISLANDS*.

SO, YOU HAVE NO LEADS?

NO WAY TO FIND OUT WHO *OWNS* CARPATHIAN INVESTMENTS, WHO *KILLED* LINDA HUNT?

CARPATHIAN IS A PRIVATE *HOLDING* COMPANY, OWNED BY A *SHELL* CORPORATION, WHOLLY CONTROLLED BY AN INVESTMENT FUND ORGANIZED AS A *BLIND TRUST*--

ACTUALLY, WE DO HAVE *ONE* LEAD.

A *PHONE NUMBER* ON CARPATHIAN'S CAYMAN ISLAND INCORPORATION PAPERS.

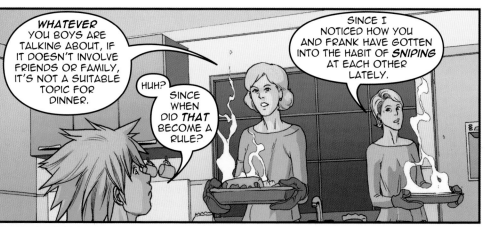

WHATEVER YOU BOYS ARE TALKING ABOUT, IF IT DOESN'T INVOLVE FRIENDS OR FAMILY, IT'S NOT A SUITABLE TOPIC FOR DINNER.

HUH?

SINCE WHEN DID *THAT* BECOME A RULE?

SINCE I NOTICED HOW YOU AND FRANK HAVE GOTTEN INTO THE HABIT OF *SNIPING* AT EACH OTHER LATELY.

WHAT THIS FAMILY NEEDS IS MORE *QUALITY* TIME TOGETHER.

STARTING AT THE DINNER TABLE.

AGREED?

AGREED.

AGREED.

LOVELY.

LET'S EAT.

LATER.

YOUR MOTHER'S RIGHT, YOU KNOW.

YOU BOYS HAVE BEEN AT EACH OTHER'S THROATS A *LOT* LATELY.

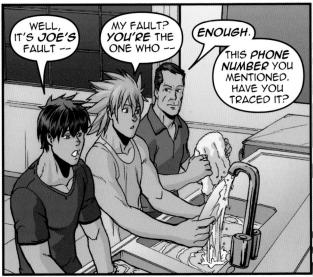

WELL, IT'S *JOE'S* FAULT --

MY FAULT? *YOU'RE* THE ONE WHO --

ENOUGH.

THIS *PHONE NUMBER* YOU MENTIONED. HAVE YOU TRACED IT?

WE DID.

IT'S THE SAME PHONE NUMBER USED BY THOSE THUGS WHO TRIED TO ROB THE BAYPORT MUSEUM USING A ZOMBIE CRAWL FOR COVER.*

REGISTERED TO A *PHONY ADDRESS* WAY OUT WEST IN *RIVER HEIGHTS.*

*SEE HARDY BOYS THE NEW CASE FILES #1.

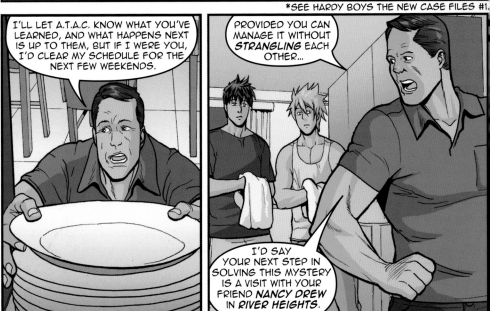

I'LL LET A.T.A.C. KNOW WHAT YOU'VE LEARNED, AND WHAT HAPPENS NEXT IS UP TO THEM, BUT IF I WERE YOU, I'D CLEAR MY SCHEDULE FOR THE NEXT FEW WEEKENDS.

PROVIDED YOU CAN MANAGE IT WITHOUT *STRANGLING* EACH OTHER...

I'D SAY YOUR NEXT STEP IN SOLVING THIS MYSTERY IS A VISIT WITH YOUR FRIEND *NANCY DREW* IN *RIVER HEIGHTS.*

TO BE CONTINUED -- IN *NANCY DREW THE NEW CASE FILES #3!*

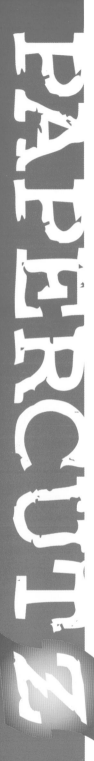

WATCH OUT FOR PAPERCUTZ™

Welcome to the second awesome volume of the all-new THE HARDY BOYS The New Case Files graphic novel series! I'm retired A.T.A.C. agent Jim Salicrup, Editor-in-Chief of Papercutz, publisher of graphic novels for all-ages. Generally, this page is devoted to getting you all the latest news from Papercutz—letting you know what's going on in many of the other great Papercutz graphic novels. Since there's so much to tell, we're going to run through all the exciting announcements as fast as we can, and try to squeeze as much as possible onto this page!

BIONICLE #9 "The Fall of Atero" – It's "The BIONICLE Glatorian saga!" This is perhaps the most action-packed graphic novel series ever published by Papercutz! If you're familiar with the BIONICLE, but never seen the comics—what are you waiting for?! Written by Greg Farshtey, illustrated by Pop Mhan.

CLASSICS ILLUSTRATED #12 "The Island of Dr. Moreau" – This is the graphic novel series that takes stories by the world's greatest authors and adapts them into comics. H. G. Wells's tragic tale of monstrous mutants is brought to dark life by writer Steven Grant, and artist Eric Vincent.

DISNEY ADVENTURES #5 "Tinker Bell and the Pirate Adventure" – Now in the same bigger format as HARDY BOYS THE NEW CASE FILES! Think life is easy in Never Land? Then you've probably forgot all about Captain Hook! He's back, along with his pirates, to disrupt the lives of Tinker Bell, Terence, and the other fairies. Giulia Conti, Augusto Machetto, & Paola Mulazzi, writers; Gianluca Barone,Andrea Greppi, Elisabetta Melaranci, & Emilio Urbano, artists.

PAPERCUTZ SLICES
AN ALL-NEW, UNAUTHORIZED PARODY
breaking down
STEFAN PETRUCHA & RICK PARKER
PAPERCUTZ

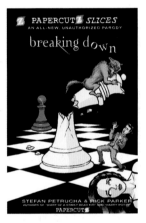

GERONIMO STILTON #7 "Dinosaurs in Action" – Geronimo and friends travel all the way back in time to the Cretaceous Period to rescue Professor Von Volt from the Pirate Cats! If that wasn't tough enough, a few dinosaurs make matters positively dangerous!

TALES FROM THE CRYPT #9 "Wickeder" – Glugg, the Stinky Dead Kid is back in an all-new story by Margo Kinney-Petrucha & Stefan Petrucha, writers; Diego Jourdan, artist. Plus "Kill, Baby, Kill!" by Scott Lobdell, writer; James Romberger & Marguerite Van Cook, artists. Gross and creepy comics with a twisted sense of humor!

PAPERCUTZ SLICES #2 "Breaking Down" – The unofficial parody of the Twilight series, as sliced up by Maia Kinney-Petrucha, Stefan Petrucha, writers; Rick Parker, artist.

THE SMURFS #5 "The Smurfs and the Egg" – A magic egg, one that can grant any wish, throws the Smurf Village into turmoil! If that wasn't enough, the evil sorcerer Gargamel has concocted a potion that turns him into "The Fake Smurf"! Yvan Delporte & Peyo, writers; Peyo, artist.

And if that's not enough graphic novels to keep you entertained 'till Summer, you must check out NANCY DREW The New Case Files #2 "Vampire Slayer" Part Two (Check out the preview on the following pages)! Why? The answer is that parts one and two of "Vampire Slayer," as well as THE HARDY BOYS The New Case Files #1 and #2 all lead into NANCY DREW The New Case Files #3 "Together with The Hardy Boys"!

Yes, at long last, due to popular demand, Nancy Drew and The The Hardy Boys finally team-up in a graphic novel! But it's a team-up like you've never seen before—Frank and Joe Hardy no longer want to work together, and Ned Nickerson has left Nancy Drew. With all these personal conflicts how can the teen detectives hope to solve one of their biggest mysteries ever? Whatever you do, don't miss NANCY DREW The New Case Files #3 "Together with The Hardy Boys," written by Gerry Conway and drawn by Sho Murase! Be sure to check www.papercutz.com for further details.

Till then, watch out for Papercutz!

Thanks, Jim

Available Now . . .

Nancy Drew © 2011 Simon & Schuster

Nancy Drew must stop a woman determined to destroy a vampire -- Gregor Coffson! But why? Has the Girl Detective fallen under the vampire's spell? Don't miss the shock-filled conclusion to "Vampire Slayer."

Still available:
"Vampire Slayer" Part I!

6x9, 64 pages, full-color. $6.99 PB, $10.99 HC. On sale at booksellers everywhere.
Or order from us. Please add $4.00 postage and handling plus $1.00 for each additional book. Please make check payable to NBM Publishing. Send to: PAPERCUTZ, 1200 Country Rd. Rte. 523, Flemington, NJ, 08822. (1-800-886-1223)

www.papercutz.com

Special preview of NANCY DREW The New Case Files #2 "Vampire Slayer" Part Two!

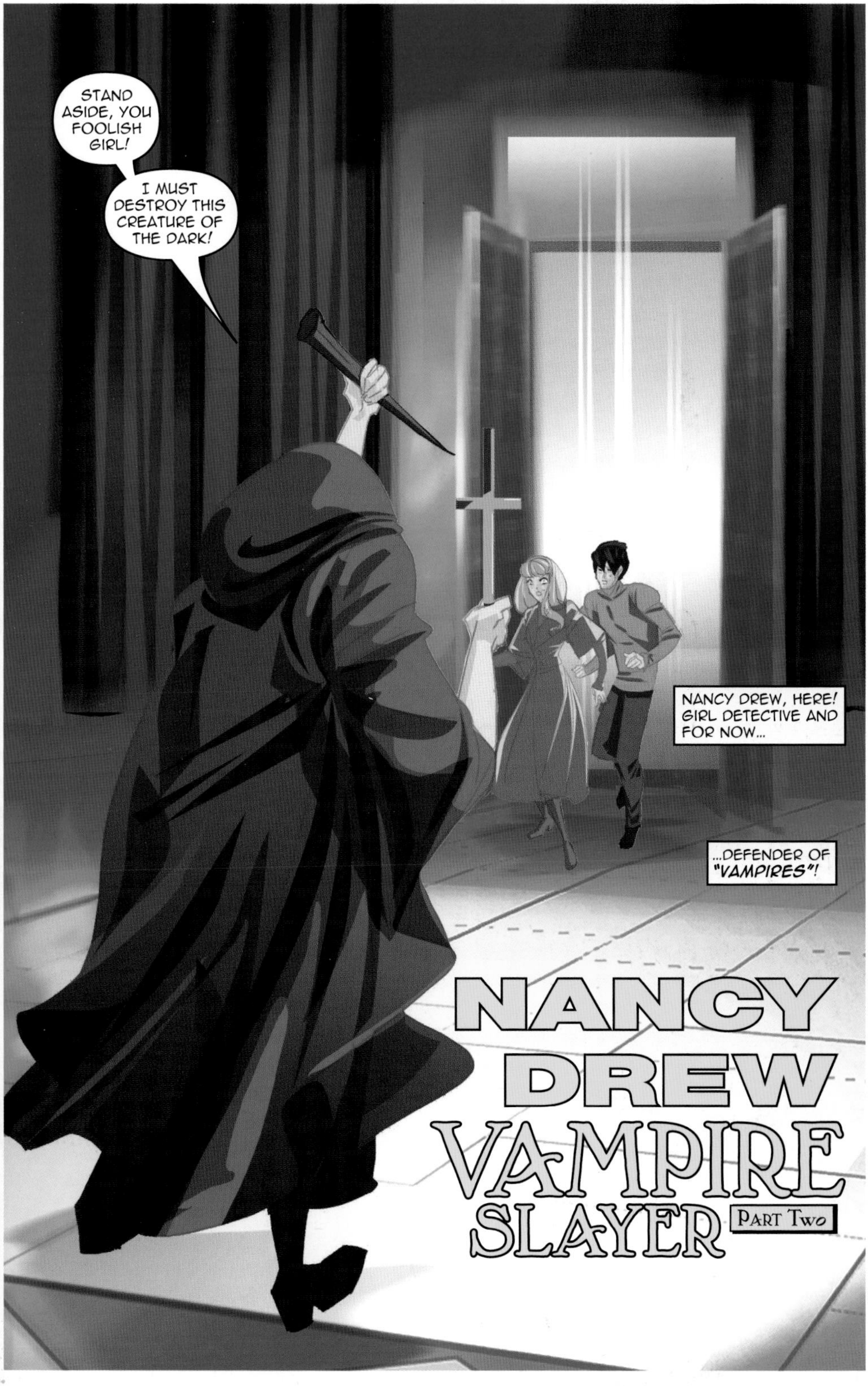
STAND ASIDE, YOU FOOLISH GIRL!
I MUST DESTROY THIS CREATURE OF THE DARK!
NANCY DREW, HERE! GIRL DETECTIVE AND FOR NOW...
...DEFENDER OF "VAMPIRES"!
NANCY DREW
VAMPIRE SLAYER
PART TWO

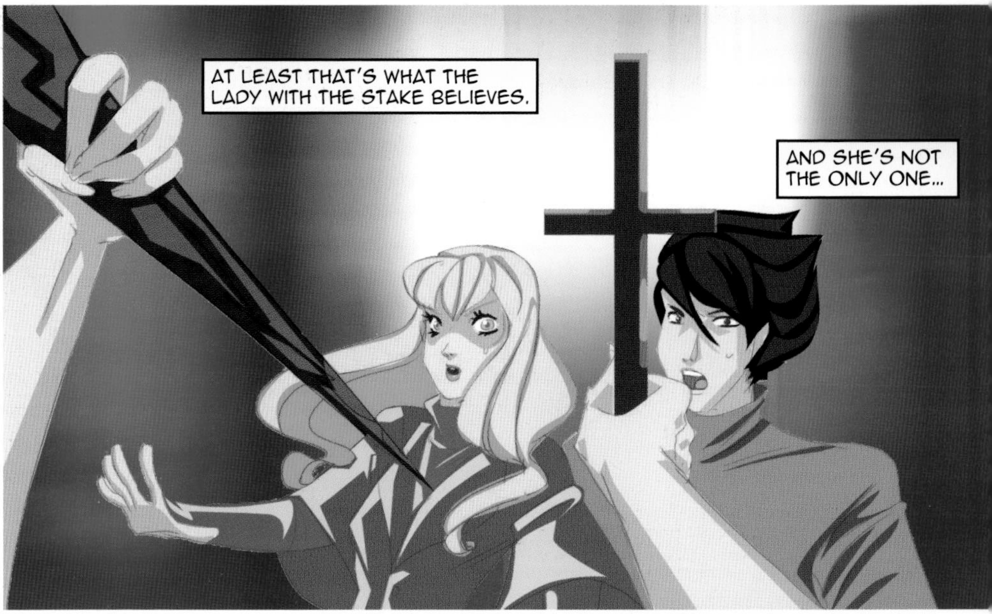
AT LEAST THAT'S WHAT THE LADY WITH THE STAKE BELIEVES.
AND SHE'S NOT THE ONLY ONE...

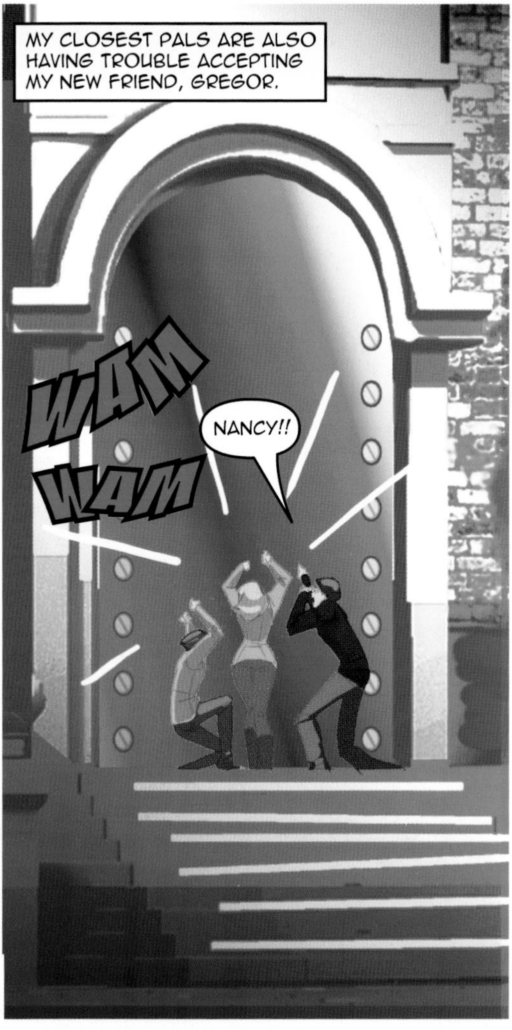
MY CLOSEST PALS ARE ALSO HAVING TROUBLE ACCEPTING MY NEW FRIEND, GREGOR.
WAM
WAM
NANCY!!

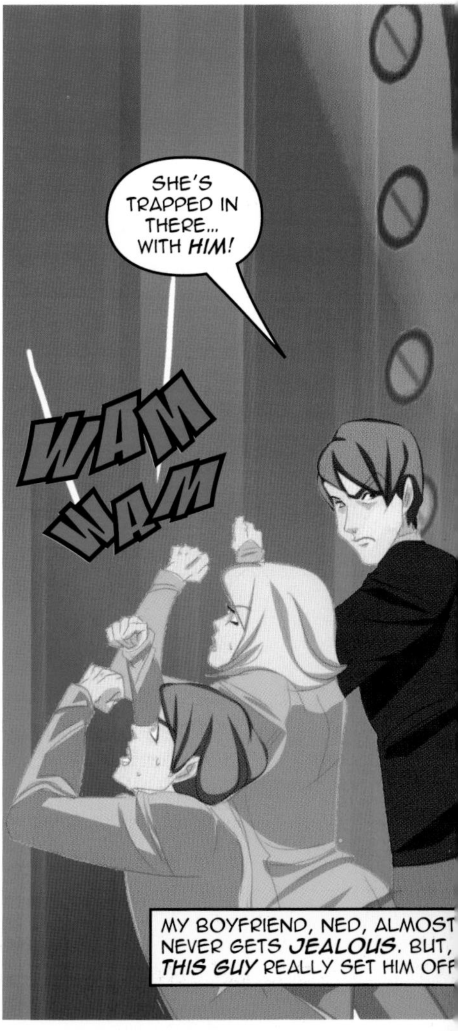
SHE'S TRAPPED IN THERE... WITH *HIM*!
WAM
WAM
MY BOYFRIEND, NED, ALMOST NEVER GETS ***JEALOUS***. BUT, ***THIS GUY*** REALLY SET HIM OFF

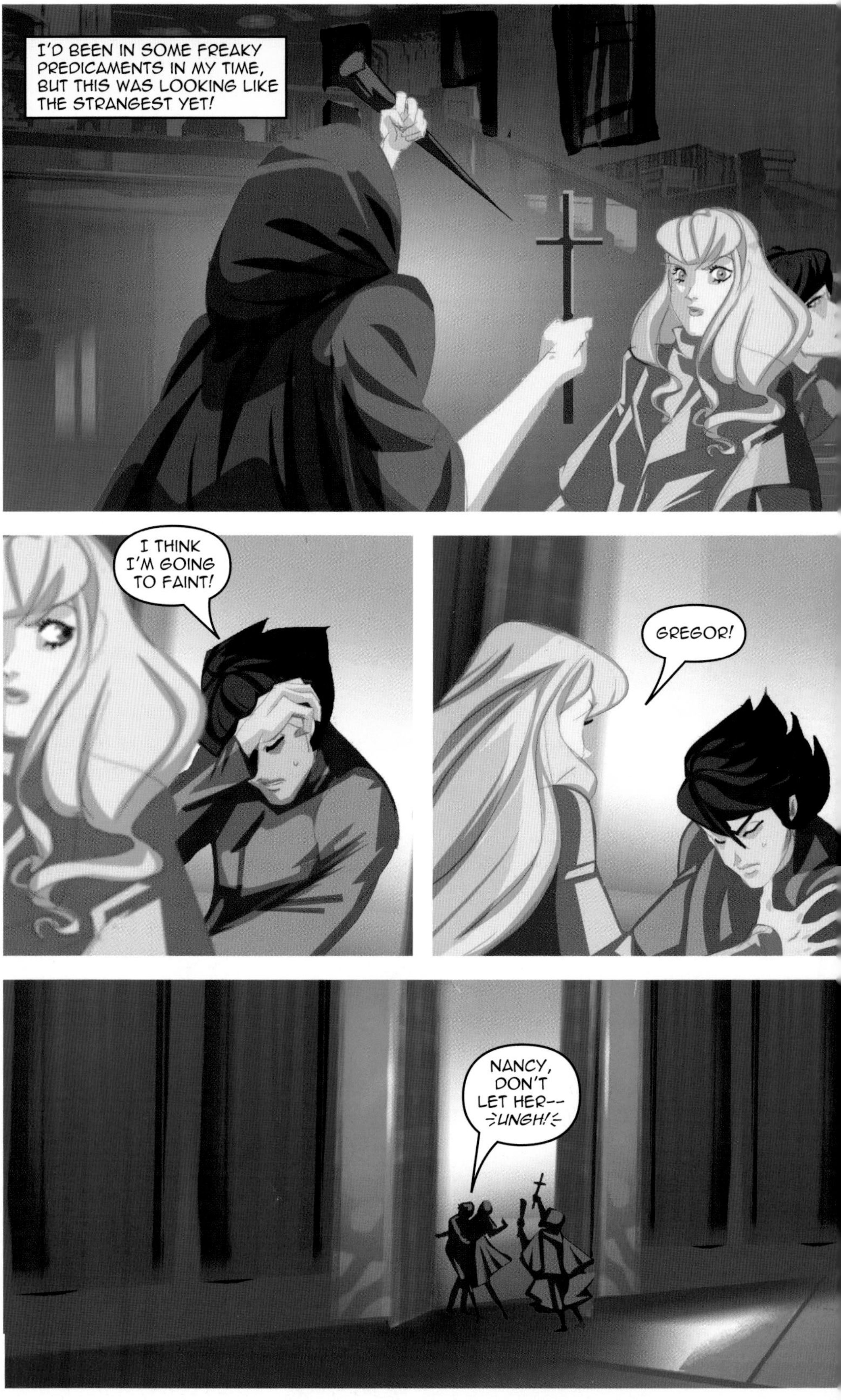
I'D BEEN IN SOME FREAKY PREDICAMENTS IN MY TIME, BUT THIS WAS LOOKING LIKE THE STRANGEST YET!
I THINK I'M GOING TO FAINT!
GREGOR!
NANCY, DON'T LET HER-- UNGH!

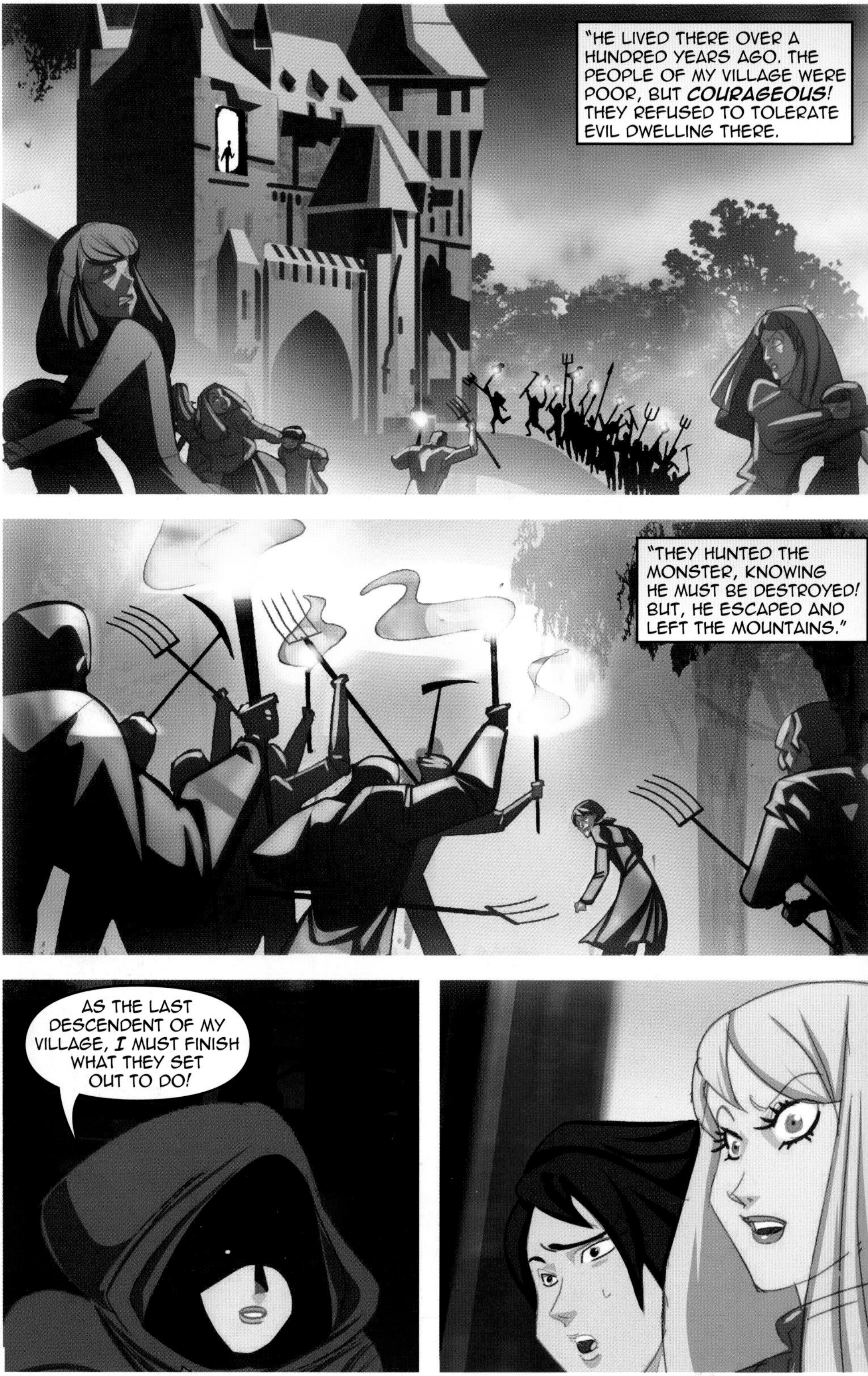
"HE LIVED THERE OVER A HUNDRED YEARS AGO. THE PEOPLE OF MY VILLAGE WERE POOR, BUT COURAGEOUS! THEY REFUSED TO TOLERATE EVIL DWELLING THERE.
"THEY HUNTED THE MONSTER, KNOWING HE MUST BE DESTROYED! BUT, HE ESCAPED AND LEFT THE MOUNTAINS."
AS THE LAST DESCENDENT OF MY VILLAGE, I MUST FINISH WHAT THEY SET OUT TO DO!

Get the complete story in NANCY DREW The New Case Files #2 "Vampire Slayer" Part Two - Available at booksellers everywhere!

Who is behind the strange occurrences in River Heights and Bayport?

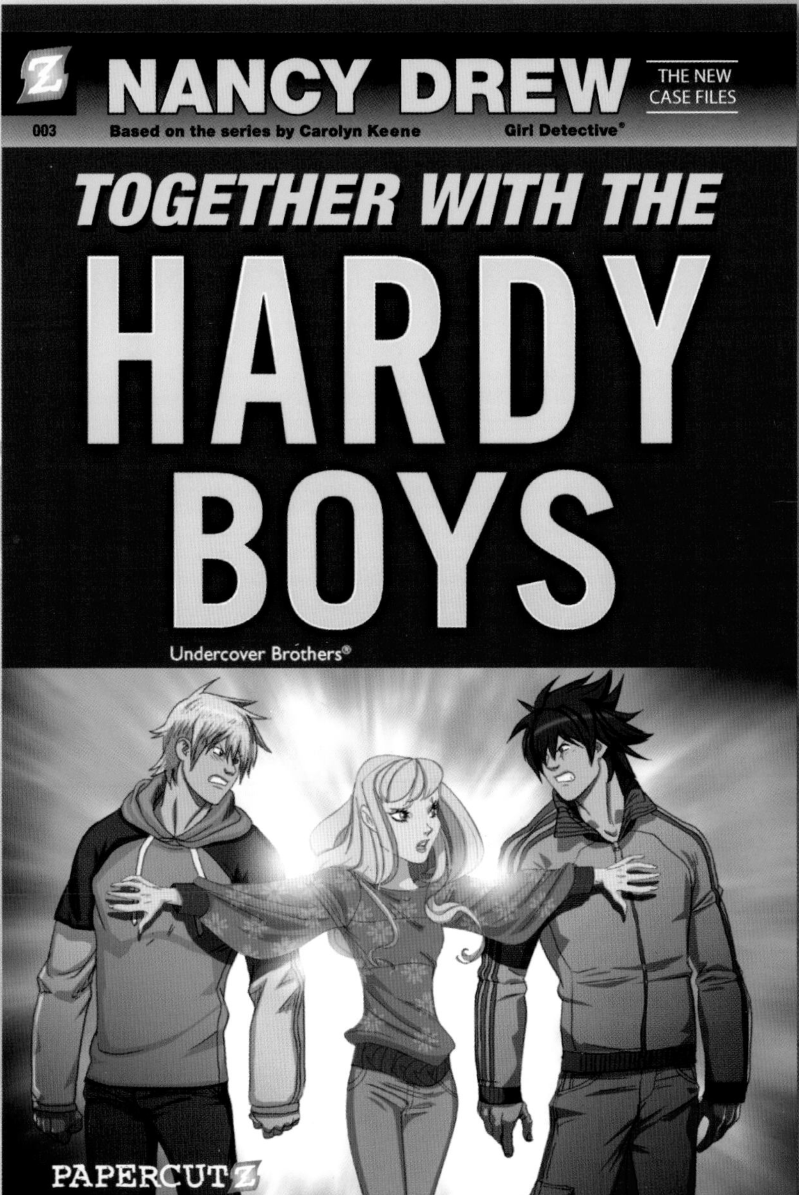

NANCY DREW
THE NEW CASE FILES
003
Based on the series by Carolyn Keene
Girl Detective®
TOGETHER WITH THE
HARDY BOYS
Undercover Brothers®
PAPERCUTZ

Can Nancy Drew keep Joe and Frank together long enough to find out? Don't miss this thrilling conclusion to the storylines from THE HARDY BOYS and NANCY DREW!

COMING AUGUST 2011